Behind
Closed
Doors

A.L. Smith

Behind Closed Doors

Breaking the Line Books Small Press
Copyright © 2015 by A.L. Smith

ISBN-13: 978-0-692-53469-4

This title is also available in e-book through Amazon Kindle and other retail outlets.

Visit www.alsmithbooks.com for more information.

Library of Congress Control Number: 2015951964

Printed in the United States of America

Dedication Zeth Blaimes Garrison

Acknowledgements

Before all others, I have to give thanks to the Almighty, who is without a doubt, the true author and finisher of my course.
To my parents, Lorenza and Mary Smith, thank you for giving me life and the ability to think outside of the box.
To my siblings, Rodney, Tosha, Anika (aka Amina Dyamond) and Kiana, I love you to the moon and back.

To my grandparents, Rosie & Willie Latin and Blaimes Smith, Sr., may you rest in peace and to Doris Smith, the last one standing, each of you gave me the gift of perpetual motivation and the audacity to believe.

To Uncle Jimmy, you had me convinced that I could do anything, and my Uncle Blaimes Smith, Jr, you once told me, "everything you touch turns to gold"...THANK YOU (smile).

To Sandra Kaye Boone, in the midst of your storm, you saw my vision and you took the time to encourage me.

To all of my friends and surrogate moms (you know who you are) what's understood never has to be explained, nor will it be forgotten.

Peace,
A.L. Smith

Prologue

Sierra

"Sierra, why did you let him do that to you?"
After finally getting the nerve to tell her that my cousin Keith was a perverted pedophile, this was her response. I looked at my mother in total disbelief. Like most victims, I kept quiet because I was ashamed and thought it was my fault. I was convinced that I must have done something to provoke him. Protecting the abuser and sparing other family members from the pain of knowing such a horrible thing is typical behavior for abused children according to Oprah and Dr. Phil. Apparently, my mother hadn't got the memo.

"If what you're saying is true, then why didn't you tell someone?"
She glared at me as if I was the villain and not the victim. Really? This was exactly the reason I never said anything.

I was four when my nightmare began and Keith around fourteen or fifteen. He lived with us off and on for reasons that weren't really clear at first. He would just show up at our house in the middle of the night and stay for long periods of time. Our house was actually my grandparent's home. It was also home to many other family members who were down on their luck and needed a place to stay. There were times when we had three or four people to a bed. My grandparents never turned anyone away. At some point, I discovered Keith was the firstborn illegitimate son of a close relative on my grandfather's side of the family and my grandfather treated him like a son. Apparently, his mother married someone other than Keith's

4

father and started a family. I figured Keith just didn't fit in. When he was no longer welcomed in his mother's home, he came to live with us. The situation gave Keith complete access to me, and from time to time, my cousins as well.

I often wonder how I ended up on a path that would lead me to the dark and empty places that became my existence. I was born on July 2, 1975. I never knew my father, but it didn't become an issue until I started school. I cringed whenever the teacher did the little mommy and daddy scenarios. I went home and asked questions, but I never got an answer. At some point it became a non-issue. No one talked about it and neither did I. In my heart, I believed Carl was my father because I looked just like his mother Ruby. She was a frail, petite looking lady with a perfect nose and beautiful hair. I had all of her features. My mom and I actually ran into Carl in the grocery store once and after staring at me for a moment, he looked at my mother and said, "She's mine, isn't she?" My mother gave me a nervous look and tried to laugh it off.

"Answer me," he demanded. I just stood there frozen and speechless, waiting for her response. Carl never took his eyes off of me. She finally sent me on a scavenger hunt for items that were not on the shopping list. I'm sure she did it in order to exclude me from the conversation that she was having with Carl. As we left the store, I could see the sadness in his eyes. I'm not sure how the conversation actually went but I never saw him again. Eventually, I gave up and resigned myself to the fact that I would never know.

By the time I reached middle school, I was convinced that every little girl had a cousin like Keith. I can still remember each and every experience as if it was only yesterday. I can also remember exactly where my mother was each time it happened. She was never far away. And she had the nerve to blame me?

I came to Las Vegas for a lot of reasons, but staying never really made sense. I'm 33-years old with two kids and no future. I got pregnant during my senior year in high school and managed to hide it until my seventh month. Damarcus was born a few weeks after my high school graduation and quickly became an added joy to our family. After graduation, I followed in my mother's footsteps and attended community college. My plan was to become a registered nurse. However, I dropped out after the first semester. Even though my mom and my grandmother were built in babysitters, I quit because I wanted to stay home with my son. Well that was the story that I told everyone. In reality, I quit various other reasons. For one, I just didn't fit in. I'd always felt unattractive, even in high school, but amidst the more sophisticated college girls, my negative self-image was far worse. And even though I graduated from high school with honors, I was also intimidated by the class work. My main reason for quitting was because I had other plans. Damien, my son's father, had joined the Marines and was supposed to come back for me and Demarcus. He was going places and I thought he was gonna take me. That was my reason for getting pregnant in the first place. Of course, it never happened. A couple of years went by before I realized he wasn't coming back, at least not for me. So with one semester of nursing school under my belt, I became an elderly companion. It paid the bills but I hated it. I would work for a while and quit after I had some money saved or a man to take care of me.

Before I knew it, I was pregnant again. Tray was definitely a surprise and like my mother, I never pretended to know who his father was. There was Ray, Jonathan, Calvin, Tim, and Jarvis. Tray resembled Jarvis more than the others, so I picked him. A few months after Tray was born, Jarvis was killed in a car accident. I didn't rejoice over his death, but in a twisted sort of way it resolved my issues regarding paternity. Tray's father was officially dead and no one could dispute it.

When I was around nineteen, I told my family about Keith. Telling them had never crossed my mind before because Keith had convinced me early on that no one would believe me. But on that particular day, I didn't care if anyone believed me or not. I had to say something. Everyone was gathered outside under my grandmother's shaded tree and I was lying on the sofa trying to take a nap. I had just found out I was pregnant with Tray and I was extremely depressed. I woke up to find Keith standing over me with his pants hanging down to his ankles. It had been a few years since our last encounter, so I was really shocked by his behavior. By then, he was an unemployed college graduate with a baby by one of our distant cousins. For whatever reason, I thought he had changed or moved on to the next victim. Guess I should've known better. The ability to appear normal and the charming personality were hallmark characteristics of a sexual predator, yet no one in my family seemed to notice. They loved his dirty drawers.

In order to deal with the years of emotional and physical abuse, I developed selective amnesia and I mastered the art of staying away from Keith. However, on this particular day, thoughts of each and every one of my experiences came rushing back. I immediately got up and headed for the front door. While pulling up his, he nearly landed on his ass as he reached out to grab me. I pushed him away with so much force that he actually ended up face down on the floor. He had this wicked grin on his face that made my flesh crawl.

"Where do you think you're going?"

"To let everyone know you're nothing but a sick ass child molester," I snapped.

"And you think they're gonna believe you, of all people?" he challenged me.

I thought about it for a moment. My response was, "probably not," and then I screamed. It took less than thirty seconds for my family to make their way into the house. By then, I was in tears but I was still able to tell them everything. When I was finally finished purging myself and recounting all of the horrible details, everyone was speechless. After what seemed like an eternity, the least likely person in the whole group spoke first. It was Keith's mother.

"Why, Keith?"

She didn't ask if he was guilty, she simply asked "why?"

Everyone looked at her as Keith looked at the floor. Suddenly it all made sense. His mom must have known about his sick attraction for little girls all along. Incredible, I thought, trying to put everything into perspective. If she knew her son was capable of such horrible things, why didn't she do something to protect us? The silence was uncomfortably thick, and then all of a sudden my grandmother made a statement that was barely audible, but I heard her.

"Aw shucks, y'all stop all this nonsense. That boy is just like his granddaddy. Peabody was the same way."

I couldn't believe it! Just like that he was justified. Recalling a scene from *The Color Purple*, I guess Miss Sophia was right when she said, "a girl child just ain't safe in a family of men…"

"Sure was," my grandmother's sister chimed in.

Finally, my mother spoke.

"Sierra, how could you let him do that to you?"

This would become one of the worst days of my life. It is permanently etched in my mind and replayed on a daily basis. I never know when the thoughts will come and I haven't determined a specific trigger. The images just suddenly appear and I'm held captive by my own mind until they fade away.

Latrice

Damn, this is my last rock and I only had two dollars to my name, I thought as I made preparations for my early morning ritual. My daily routine included hitting the pipe when I woke up and figuring out how to get enough money for my next hit. As I came down from the instant high and the rush that I just couldn't seem to live without, I considered my options and decided it was time for me to make a home visit.

My son J.T. hadn't lived with me since he was three years old. My mom took him away when it became obvious that I was an unfit mother. I visited from time to time but usually my visits were two-fold: to see my son, but most importantly it was an opportunity to hit my folks up for cash. They never turned me down and that was probably because I was a considerate crack head. I didn't steal from my family and I didn't ask them for money every day the way most of my friends did their families. I guess you could say it's a quarterly thing. About every three or four months, I was good for at least a hundred dollars. I figured it was better than nickel and diming them to death. I was pretty sure they preferred it that way and sometimes I felt like they were paying me to stay away. *"Out of sight out of mind."* Whatever, as long as they kept me on the payroll.

I've been doing this for at least twenty years. I thought about quitting when my brother died at the age of thirty from a massive heart attack, but in the end I managed to rationalize myself right back on the pipe. I was convinced that Donald had a bad heart and that was what killed him. It was the only thing that made sense because we smoked from the same pipe on the night that he died. I must have been right because Donald died years ago and I'm still here--still getting high.

I was totally submerged in my thoughts when I finally reached my destination. What the hell was going on? Ten cars in my grandmother's driveway and loud talking usually meant there was a new family "emergency." At least I knew it wasn't about me this time around. I'd been drama free for a minute. I eased my way into the living room and quietly took a seat.

Whenever I made my visits, I got the third degree about everything under the sun: where have I been, what was I planning to do about my son J.T, and my favorite, don't you think that it's time for you to get off that stuff? Thankfully, Sierra was the hot topic this time. Apparently, she was missing. Another Sierra episode, why was I not surprised? That girl was always into something. I mean damn, I knew I was messed up but who goes halfway across the country with nothing but ass and face? If that wasn't a stupid move, then I don't know what is.

But then again, Sierra had a few demons of her own. Most of my family was in the dark about a lot of things when it came to Sierra. However, I had firsthand knowledge. I found out about Keith and Sierra during my freshman year in high school. Up until that point, I never had a clue. I walked into my grandmother's room one evening after school and found them alone. When I opened the door, the first thing I saw was Keith. He was sitting on the bed with his back to the bedroom door. I knew something was wrong because I could see his facial expression in the mirror that was situated directly across from the bed. And then, I saw Sierra. After all these years, I still can't explain what happened next. Instead of running out of the house screaming bloody murder, I walked into the room and closed the door.

"Keith, what the hell do you think you're doing?"

"What does it look like I'm doing?"

"You sick bastard. I thought you changed. Looks like you just moved on."

"Are you jealous?"

"Jealous? Are you serious? I should have put your ass on blast a long time ago.

"Sierra, get your stuff and let's go."

"Sierra, don't forget what I told you…" Keith said, as Sierra scrambled to gather her things.

"What? Are you threatening her? She's a baby!! Your ass is going to jail!"

"Whatever Latrice," Keith said dismissively.

"Sierra, keep your mouth shut and remember what I told you."

Grinning, he collected his belongings and left the room.

Sierra was in tears. When she finally stopped crying, I asked her how long Keith had been messing with her.

"Since before kindergarten," she sniffed.

I did the math. She'd just turned 10 which meant she had to be at least 4. It had been six years since he stopped bothering me. And here I was thinking he'd changed. Sick bastard. I should have known better.

"Sierra, he hasn't….?"

I couldn't even say the words.

"No, but he keeps talking about it. I'm scared."

"We're telling your momma. This has to stop."

"No Latrice. I'm not telling her anything. I shouldn't have to. And if you tell her, I'm going to say you're making it all up".

"But Sierra….."

"I mean it, Latrice. It's all my fault. I should have said something the first time it happened, but I didn't. Now it's too late. No one will believe me".

"That's not true Sierra. They'll believe you if I tell them what he did to me."

"No! I swear, if you say anything, I'll deny it Latrice. Now leave me alone," she screamed.

She ran from my grandmother's room and into the room that she shared with her mother.

I sat there for a moment, trying to figure out what to do. She was right. Even if we both confessed, they probably wouldn't believe us. And if they did believe us, they would probably blame us for not speaking up sooner. A few minutes later, I heard my mother's car approach on the gravel point road. I made the fatal decision to respect Sierra's wishes and keep my mouth shut.

A couple of years later, I noticed a drastic change in Sierra. She was far more withdrawn than before and the angry outbursts toward Aunt Birdie were getting worse. Sierra never told me it happened, I just knew. The inevitable had finally occurred.

"Sierra, you have to tell your mom. He's never gonna stop."

"I can't, Latrice."

She just sat there staring into space trying to figure out the best way to end her pain. At that moment, I wanted Keith dead and I was actually thinking of ways to kill him. But Sierra wouldn't budge. She was determined to keep this secret forever. Eventually, I gave up. However, I made a point to pray for Sierra every night. I also prayed that Keith would die a slow tortuous death.

As I entered my sophomore year, I was determined to put it all behind me once and for all. By this time, all of my friends were sexually active. While I'd never gone all the way, I was far more advanced than all of them combined. After my first experience with a guy named Casey from my homeroom class,

I became the most popular girl in our class. I'm pretty sure my popularity was due to my willingness to have sex with just about anyone bold enough to ask, however, I chose to believe otherwise. I kept telling myself it was all due to the fact that I was prettier and cooler than all the other girls. They were just square. Somehow, I still managed to get decent enough grades, but I was tired of the school scene. Eventually, I started skipping school and hanging out with an older crowd. This was perhaps the biggest mistake I ever made in my life.

At first, it was just alcohol. Next, it was weed. According to all the fancy research studies, weed is the proverbial "gateway" drug. Guess what? They were right. I smoked my first rock in the summer of 1986. While hanging out at the skating rink, I met an older guy who was clearly out of place for such an immature scene. We connected immediately and things got moving pretty fast. We bounced before closing time and headed for his souped up '78 Cutlass, which was complete with chrome rims and tinted windows. Oddly, he didn't pick up on the fact that I was adventurous and enjoyed all things pertaining to sex, even with a complete stranger. Had he picked up on this little piece of information, perhaps he never would have offered me a hit on his crack pipe. Once again, curiosity kicked in. I wanted to try something new. In return for my generosity and expertise, he showed me the proper way to operate a crack pipe and the rest was history. I dropped out of school and headed down the long path to nowhere.

Sierra on the other hand seemed to be doing okay at this point, in spite of the circumstances. She was in junior high school getting good grades, doing science projects, and going to Sunday school every Sunday. She was still as quiet as always and well behaved except for those times when she became extremely violent toward her mother. For no apparent she would get angry and start kicking and scratching Aunt Birdie like a demon possessed. No one in the family could come up with an answer as to why she behaved that way, however, Alex and I knew.

A few years ago Alex got us all together to talk about Keith. She was seeing a shrink off and on trying to deal with the past. Apparently, she had a theory that would explain why we were all screwed up. According to Alex and her shrink, our experiences with Keith, which "occurred during our formative years," had somehow caused us to "adopt coping mechanisms to guard against our feelings of fear and distrust." Really? I couldn't believe Alex was actually paying someone to give her bogus information. I thought she was smarter than that. Well, she could fall for that psychological crap if she wanted to, but I wasn't buying it. In my humble opinion, I'm an unemployed crack head because of the choices I made. Sierra was in Vegas doing God knows what because that's what she wanted to do. And Alex couldn't keep a man because she probably didn't want one.

Alex

As a child I wanted to please everyone and I wanted everyone to think I was perfect, especially my parents. Contrary to popular belief, strict parenting is not a sure-fire way to produce perfect, well-behaved children. It actually sabotages the child's ability to develop emotional and self-discipline skills, which are key to establishing healthy adult relationships. Typically, the resultant outcome of over-restrictive parenting is rebellion.

When I reached high school, the rebellion began to rise at the same rate of speed as my hormones. Needless to say, my imperfections began to show. Lying and scheming to get out of the house became second nature for me and I was extremely good at it. It finally came to an end when my mother caught me coming in late on a school night. Of course she didn't buy the story I tried to give her and she immediately threatened to tell my dad. I freaked out because I just couldn't stand the thought of him finding out that I was less than perfect. In hindsight, I'm convinced that my obsession with perfection was probably the reason I never told anyone about Keith.

In the end, my mother didn't rat me out. I suppose you could say it was our little secret. However, from that moment on, she made my life a living hell. I was officially banned from talking on the phone and hanging out with my friends was out of the question. She basically treated me like a convicted felon and held me hostage so that she could see my every move. When she looked at me I could see the disgust in her eyes and if I had a dollar for every time she said, "if you bring a baby in this house, I ain't rocking it," I would be richer than Oprah. Well maybe not that rich, but I would definitely be well off. Looking back, I think she probably meant well but her tactics didn't work. It only added fuel to the fire. Instead of conforming, I just became more rebellious, more determined and definitely more creative.

By the time, I graduated from high school I felt like I was being paroled from prison or like a zoo animal being re-introduced to the wild. My first day at Gretna University kind of set the tone for the next three years of my life. Shortly after my parents dropped me off at the dorm, my new roommate arrived. We talked for a few minutes and quickly established the fact that I was country as hell and that her life's mission was to introduce me to the real world. Born and raised in East St Louis, Dana thought she knew everything there was to know about men and what they were good for. I was in complete awe as I listened to some of the stories she told me about her senior year in high school. Apparently, the majority of her time was spent being the girlfriend of one of the biggest cocaine dealers in East St Louis. She came to Gretna in a brand new 1990 Toyota Celica fully kitted with leather seats. She had all of the latest kicks, expensive watches with names I couldn't pronounce, Dooney bags, leather coats and riding boots in every color you could name. I was speechless.

"Wait Dana, are you telling me this guy bought you all of this stuff just because you were his girlfriend? I don't get it," I said noticing her Louis Vuitton luggage which was either the real thing or the best looking knock-off that I'd ever seen.

"I know you don't but if you hang with me long enough you will."

And with that, she suggested a tour of the campus to see what was popping for the night. As we made our way toward Q-Hill, the magnetism and enormous display of masculinity was intimidating yet alluring at the same time. From all indications, they were exceptionally adept in smelling new blood because they were on us like vultures. After hanging out on Q-Hill for a few hours, two of the frat brothers invited us to an off campus house party.

Before ever setting foot on the campus of Gretna, I promised myself that I would not get played or "turned out" like a lot of the freshmen girls I'd heard about. But there I was on day number one in a wonderful position to do just that. Luckily for me the young man that I hooked up with was a complete gentleman. Dana's friend Dee-Dog was not. Dee-Dog was actually one of the rowdiest Ques on the yard and the biggest womanizer, even though he had a steady girlfriend. I spent the evening playing Super Mario Brothers with a guy named Ken. I was totally exhausted from the excitement of my first day of freedom, so I was relieved when he finally saved the princess. I was literally falling asleep on the sofa and all I could think about was getting back to the dorm so that I could curl up in my new bed. But realizing the compromising position I was in with no car and no one I could call for a ride, I fought to stay awake. At some point, I lost the fight and woke up in the middle of Ken's king sized waterbed. Surprisingly, Ken was still fully dressed. He fell asleep on top of the covers behind me with an arm draped across my waist.

Dana, on the other hand, hooked up with a guy who was the complete opposite. I was awakened by frightening sounds coming from the other room. In a panic I tried to awaken Ken to see if he would go next door to investigate.

"Ken, wake up!"

I whispered loudly with very little response from Ken.

"Ken, what the hell is going on over there?"

I said it louder this time, shaking him as my tone escalated.

Finally I got a response, however, he didn't appear to be overly concerned. In spite of the darkness, I was able to see his finger as it approached my lips.

"Shhh," he whispered softly and slowly sat up.

"Listen," he said calmly.

As I followed his directions and listened closer, I understood his lack of concern.

"It's okay, Alex. Trust me, your friend is a willing participant in whatever they're doing in there."

Of course, he was right. I was completely embarrassed by my inadvertent display of immaturity.

"Go back to sleep sweetie," he said placing a kiss on my forehead while we assumed our former positions.

He went back to sleep immediately. I spent the rest of the night trying to imagine what the hell was going on next-door, and more specifically, what was he doing to cause her to make such noises?

The next morning Dana acted as if nothing out of the ordinary had taken place. When she emerged from Dee's bedroom, her hair stood straight up on her head, one fake eyelash was gone and all of her fake nails were missing except one. I couldn't wait to get the details.

I learned a lot from Dana before her hasty departure from Gretna. She got busted by the feds for transporting drugs to Louisiana. Dana was not just the girlfriend of the drug dealer back home. She was his number one mule. Her arrest occurred in the middle of our sophomore year. By then, we had mastered the art of partying, making it to class on time, and getting decent grades. I was really sad for her because I knew about her rough childhood. In her mind, she was doing what she needed to do to get ahead. I pointed out to her many times that if she studied a little harder she could get an academic scholarship to pay for school. But according to her, tuition was the least of her worries. She had two younger sisters and a brother at home. Without her, they would have nothing.

"Alex, I trust you. You're the only real friend I have in the whole world. I'm probably gonna have to do some time so I need someone to look after my peeps. I have enough money in this account to take care of my family for about two years. This is the checkbook for the account, my grandmother's name and address, and the amount to make the check out for each month." This conversation took place the night before her arrest, which was imminent, according to one of her homies back in East Saint Louis. She'd decided not to run. Instead, she just wanted to do her time so that she could move on with her life. When I saw the amount of money in the account, I tried to refuse.

"Dana, I can't do this. Do you know how much money you have in this damn account?"

It was eighty three thousand dollars and thirty-seven cents to be exact.

"Yes, I know how much is in there. I listen to the way you talk about your grandmother and the things you want to do for her one day, so I know you'll do the right thing. If you ever need anything, just take it. You're the only person on this earth I can trust to do this.

I did it for almost three years instead of just two. I guess Dana expected me to pay myself, but I didn't. As a result, the money lasted much longer than Dana expected. I looked forward to writing the check every month because I knew it was being put to good use. I couldn't wait to do something like that for my grandmother. Dana was sentenced to six years in federal prison for her participation in the drug ring. She could have gotten less time but she refused to testify against her boyfriend. We kept in touch via mail and she seemed to be making good on her promise to have her degree by the time she was paroled.

After Dana left, I went through a period of depression but I eventually got back to my old self. I managed to make every major campus party and I had decent enough grades to keep my parents happy. Reality set in when I entered my third year of college. I needed to make straight A's in the remainder of my classes, if I really planned on getting into law school. It was definitely an ambitious goal, but I had no choice. Another strange thing happened that year. I got saved - re-baptized and everything. Once known as a party girl on campus and by this time sorority girl, everyone was surprised when my demeanor and conversation completely changed. During that time, I found myself reflecting on the past more than ever before. I was tired of living my life to please other people. My heart had been broken more times than I could count and I was searching for something that I would never find in a relationship. By instinctively placing everyone else's feelings before my own, I was literally playing Russian roulette with my life. Up until that point, I had managed to suppress a lot of my past by pretending it never happened. However, it didn't take a master's degree in psychology to know that my poor self-regard and self-value was directly related to my childhood experiences.

"Read Romans 10:9."

This was my message to everyone who would listen. I'd seen the light and I wanted everyone else to see it too. The only two people that actually listened were my baby sister and my uncle, who was a life-long alcoholic. They were genuinely interested in what I had to say and they didn't criticize me for the drastic change in my behavior. I prayed every day for forgiveness and I thanked God for what I considered a second chance.

Then out of the blue, Titus re-entered my life. Titus was a sexy chocolate brother from New York who could have been the spokesperson for S-Curl. Unfortunately, he was very much aware of his outward appeal to women and he used it to his advantage. I met him at the beginning of my sophomore year before Dana got busted and she warned me about him. However, her warning was a little late. By then I was absolutely smitten with him, but thanks to Dana's "training" I never let him know it. Instead, I just hung out with him sporadically because it was easier than setting myself up for a broken heart. After swearing off men until I got married, Titus moved into the off-campus apartment directly across from me. How the heck does that happen? It had to be the devil. The temptation finally got the best of me. I was totally weak and absolutely incapable of saying no to him. Before I knew it, I was back on the roller coaster. After a few weeks of total indulgence I was finally able to let him go for good. I spent the rest of my time at Gretna in repentance, trying really hard to do the right thing.

Chapter One

Alex

"Attorney Phillips, you have a call on line one. It's your mom."

Great, let me guess, another family crisis. She never calls me at work unless there's an "emergency". I always dreaded these calls because they brought me back to reality. My whole family is a mess and so am I.

"Hello, momma. What's going on?" I said trying to hide my irritation.

I was in the middle of my fifth revision of a closing argument for a highly publicized wrongful death case. While my position at the esteemed Kennedy, Bridgefourth, Griggs and Associates was secure, I was in fierce competition for the coveted senior partner position, which had recently become available. A win in this case, which involved a multi-million dollar settlement, would more than seal the deal for me. Closing arguments were projected to begin in two days and I couldn't afford to have any distractions, but like always, I was the sounding board and problem solver for my family whenever necessary.

"Well Patty just called and said that Birdie can't get Sierra on the phone and ain't heard from her for two weeks."

So, Sierra was the subject of our latest family emergency. I was not surprised. Out of the blue, she just picked up and moved to Vegas of all places. She'd been gone for a few years and no one knew her actual residence, occupation, or how to reach her half the time. She constantly changed her cell phone number and sent packages for her kids without a return address. I had my own ideas about what she was doing, but I kept them to myself. In a textbook sort of way, I completely understood her course of action. It was classic: low self-esteem due to abuse as a child. She was searching for something she lost a long time ago but try telling that to my family.

Sierra got the worst of it with Keith because he was always at my grandparent's house. I, on the other hand only had to deal with him sporadically. It was usually at my grandparent's house, but sometimes it was in my own home. Whoever said children from broken homes were the only ones to experience this type of indecency was sadly mistaken. I lived with both my parents and it still happened to me. My dad was mean as hell, but for some reason he liked Keith. So whenever Keith knocked on the door in the middle of the night in need of a place to stay, my dad never said no. He would sleep in the room with me and my sister never resisting the urge to take advantage of the situation. Fondling was his primary thing with me, but according to my cousins he was far more sinister than I ever could have imagined.

I must have been around four or five when it started and it went on for several years. One night, when I was around seven or eight years old, I decided I just couldn't take it anymore. When I heard the knock at the door, I knew it was him. I got up and located the sleeping bag at the top of my closet. Taking Tina, who was around four at the time, I rushed into the adjoining bathroom and locked the door. I wrapped her in the sleeping bag and lightly patted her on the back until she went back to sleep. I didn't sleep at all that night for fear that my parents would find us in the bathroom and force me to reveal the horrible secret. Somehow, Keith had managed to convince me that even though his perverted actions made me feel disgusting, it was "normal." He also told me that my parents would be mad at me instead of him if I ever told. Through fear, Keith controlled me and I hated him for it, but I think I grew to hate myself even more.

As the sun began to creep into the bathroom window that morning, I looked at Tina, who was still asleep and decided this would never happen to her. While my parents had unknowingly placed us in harm's way and ultimately failed to protect me, I was determined that he would never get his hands on Tina. Eventually, Keith stopped coming to our house. Apparently, he got the message.

Of course, I am empathetic when it comes to Sierra, but for the life of me, I can't understand how she let it ruin her life to this degree. Whatever happened to adapt and over come? As for Sierra's mother, I found it strange how some people could pick and choose which things are important to them. For instance, finding out that your child's entire childhood was ruined by a perverted family member was swept under the rug, but it was a big deal when that same child didn't want to talk to you. Go figure! The bottom line was, if anything happened to Sierra in Las Vegas everyone had to share the blame, including me.

Intermittent feelings of guilt had been as much a part of my life as breathing for as long as I could remember. However, in recent years, the guilt had become all consuming. When I brought this to my therapist's attention, she offered an array of answers and theories regarding the source of my guilt. According to her, the secrecy associated with interfamilial abuse is the greatest barrier to healing.

"It is the root cause of the overwhelming sense of shame and guilt that you're struggling to overcome. You have to face it head on, Alex, or you will never truly heal."

Chapter Two

Sierra

Ok, was he ever gonna get an erection? I'd been hooking him up for over twenty minutes and he only paid for ten. If this went on any longer, I would've owed him some change. I must be slipping. I'd never had a problem doing my job, but here lately, it was happening all the time. I knew I didn't have it going on like I did when I first came to Vegas, but I wasn't completely washed up like some of my competition.

When I first got here, I did my own thing. I wasn't about to share my money with some guy just so he could "protect" me. As an independent contractor, I handled my own business and answered to no one. Things were great for a while and then I guess my number came up. Of course, I had been warned, but I didn't listen. Janell, one of the more experienced ladies on the strip would tell me all the time "one out of every ten of your tricks is messed up in the head. You think you don't need protection, but your day is coming." She was right.

I picked up this white trick named Danny: business suit, brief case, the kind that I liked. Of course, he wanted the works and I immediately gave him my little hustle speech, which usually helped me to get the biggest bang for the buck—or vice versa.

"It's busy out there tonight and I can't afford to be holed up with you all night," I said, giving him the opening line and trying to size him up at the same time.

"Now, if you got five hundred dollars to spend, we might be able to work something out."

Before I could get the words out, I had five one hundred dollar bills in my hand and it was on. Hell, for five hundred dollars, I could get real freaky, but that wasn't really what he wanted. As soon as the lights went off, this nice, seemingly decent young man, became a beast. The first thing he did was tie my hands to the head board. This didn't really alarm me because a lot of tricks liked the rough stuff. But all of a sudden, he became violent.

"Is this what you wanted? You rotten filthy whore. I'm only giving you what you deserve," he hissed, as his face became distorted with shear hatred.

At the same time, he penetrated me with every object he could find except his own penis. When he was done, there was blood everywhere. My face was swollen and I had this horrible pain in my belly. The last thing I remember was watching him take the five hundred dollars and replace it with two one-dollar bills. I woke up in the hospital. Somehow, I managed to dial 911 before I passed out.

According to the nurse, my insides were severely damaged. Before she could finish giving me the details, the chief of gynecology walked in.

"Sir, can you please tell me what's happening? Am I going to live?" I said trying desperately to speak in spite of the radiating pain on both sides of my face.

"Yes you're going to live. We've already performed a minor procedure called dilation and curettage or D&C, in hopes of stopping the bleeding without taking you through major surgery."

He stopped speaking for a moment to make sure I was following him.

"However, you're still bleeding profusely and your blood count is declining rapidly. We need to take you to surgery for a closer look in order the find the source of the bleeding and fix it. Ma'am, there's a great possibility that we may have to remove your uterus. The procedure is called a hysterectomy," again, he hesitated. "Having your uterus removed means you will no longer have the ability to bear children."

A hysterectomy. Wow. Back home women who had hysterectomies were called "empty or hollow" and were not as desirable to men. I pondered on that for a moment, but the momentary reservation became null and void due to the excruciating pain in my belly. I simply nodded my head for fear that speaking would make the pain worse.

"By the way, ma'am," my handsome little blue-eyed doctor said, "Your baby didn't survive."

"Baby? What baby?"

I knew my period was kind of late, two months to be exact, but I figured it was due to on the job stress.

"By our estimation you were about twelve weeks pregnant. There was just too much trauma and you lost too much blood. We're amazed that you even survived".

"Could you tell if it was a boy or a girl?"

"No we couldn't, I'm sorry."

I had to look away. His eyes contained something that resembled pity, but there's a small chance it could have been disgust. Just as well, this would have been my fourth child if I had carried all of them. I brought two into the world, miscarried one with Al and now this one. Why does God allow people like me to even get pregnant when there were so many decent women who couldn't have kids?

Within minutes, I was signing consent forms as they wheeled me down the hall to the surgical suite.

"Do you have any family that we could contact for you?" the nurse asked me.

"No, but I have a friend that you could call."

I gave her Janell's number and that was the last thing I remembered. She was there when I woke up from surgery.

"Sierra, I told you..."

26

"Yeah I know. One out of ten tricks is crazy as hell," we repeated together.

"Believe me, your words rang loud and clear while that bastard was kicking my ass. You were right, I never should have been out there on my own."

"I'm glad you came to your senses, but you didn't have to lose your damn uterus in the process."

It wasn't funny, but I had to laugh to keep from crying again because she was right. I loved Janell because she was honest and the closest thing to family I've had since I left home.

"I been telling you this since the day you got here. Now, I already talked to Lenny and he said he would consider adding you to his stable. When he comes to see you, I want you to watch your mouth because everybody already thinks you're a high-falutin' ho. He says his decision will probably be based on how you heal. I didn't tell him about the hysterectomy. You know how men feel about women who ain't got no uterus. Of course, I ain't had one for five years or better and I haven't had any complaints yet. So, don't let it get you down. There's still a lot of money to be made. You need to hurry up and get well so we can go out and make some."

Janell was all of twenty-eight years old, yet she sounded like somebody's grandmother or some well- seasoned lady of the street. Come to think of it she was both. She started turning tricks for perverted old men back in Mississippi when she was fourteen years old. She had her first kid shortly thereafter. She caught a bus to Vegas on her sixteenth birthday, after her mom caught her in bed with her stepdad. When she left, she took everything she owned which included some clothes, a clock radio and a picture of Madison, her little girl.

In her letter she wrote:

"I'm leaving. I don't know where I'm going, but I will be okay. Vincent, please take care of your child. Don't let her end up like me. Momma, I'm sorry."

Vincent was very much aware of the fact that he was Madison's father. Hell, everyone in Greenwood Mississippi knew except her mom. Janell hadn't gone back since, but she heard that her mom and stepfather had worked things out and were raising Madison as their own. At first, Janell couldn't believe that her mother had chosen to stay with the man who got her fourteen year old daughter pregnant, but over the years, she'd conditioned herself not to care. She was just glad that Madison had a roof over her head and a mother and father. She prayed every night that Madison would be safe in the house with that twisted bastard. After all, she was his biological daughter. Now, thirteen years later, she was a grandmother. I was with her when she got the news. She was physically ill at the thought of her stepfather or some beer-bellied old man having sex with her baby. Thank God that was not the case. Madison's baby's father was a fellow classmate. It's amazing how we find peace in small things.

Janell left the hospital around five. She had to get a nap before she went to work. She brought Lenny to the hospital the next day as promised. No mistake about it, this guy was a piece of eye candy. He was a Creole-looking, half-gangster, half-business type brother from south Louisiana. He had soft wavy hair, greenish-brown eyes and he resembled the actor Michael Ealy from Hollywood's presentation of the Donald Goines' classic *Never Die Alone*. He was wearing a conservative little outfit: khakis and a Polo shirt, nothing like you would expect from a real pimp. However, it was his walk and his swagger that gave him away. There was no mistaking this man for anything other than a hustler. Our eyes connected as soon as he entered the room. I was the first to look away because I didn't want him to see how weak I really was. I'd read enough Iceberg Slim novels to know that pimps preyed on weak-minded women. I refused to go out like that.

Thankfully, I had gotten up and combed my hair. In spite of all the bruises I was confident that Lenny would see that I still had it going on. After the introductions, Janell politely excused herself so that we could begin the negotiation process. Lenny didn't waste any time.

"How old are you, Black?" he said with that deep south Louisiana accent.

"Twenty-eight," I lied, with a straight face.

"Where you from," he asked, looking directly into my eyes.

"Kingston", I answered quietly.

"Jamaica?"

"No. Kingston, Louisiana, not Kingston Jamaica," I said, trying not to laugh out loud.

"So you're a country girl, huh? Twenty-eight is a little old in this business, but country girls are usually good for a little more mileage than most. From my estimation, you got a few years left in the game," he said, as he peered beyond the superficial layers of my face. He was admiring the beauty that was partially hidden by the bruises, which were still in the process of healing.

"You gotta work harder than the younger ladies, Black, if you wanna retire comfortably, you heard me?"

The south Louisiana accent was unmistakable and so was his use of the endearing term, "Black." Down south, nicknames were assigned to certain individuals according to their skin tones. Dark skinned people were called "Black" and individuals with lighter skin were called "Red." I knew he was shooting game at me but I went along with it.

"I'm a hard worker, Lenny, and I'm pretty damn good at what I do."

Hesitating for a moment to gauge his reaction to my boldness, I continued my well-rehearsed speech.

"To be honest with you, I had a respectable piece of money put away before this little incident, but this hospital is probably going to get the majority of it," I lied as I sat up in the bed and put on my game face.

I didn't have enough money to pay for even the first hour of my stay at the hospital but that was my business, not his.

"Before I make any commitments, I need to know the split."

I already knew the answer, but I couldn't let him think I was green just because I was from the country.

"Fifty/fifty," he said smoothly while he played with the toothpick in his mouth.

It took a lot of doing for me to hide my surprise. The current rate on the street was sixty/forty, pimps up hoes down. Most of the girls I knew would have taken that offer with a quickness, but I had to haggle a little on the basis of general principal.

So with all of the toughness I could muster laced with just the right tone, I came right back with my trademark passive aggression.

"You know I'm not used to sharing my money with anyone. I have a lot of financial responsibilities to consider…"

His lingering gaze was almost too much for me bear. Just when I was about to concede, he made another offer, "Sixty/forty. You take sixty, I'll take forty."

I almost choked on the glass of water I was drinking. Somehow, I had just managed to bluff the coldest pimp in Vegas. For a fleeting moment, I did a few mental cartwheels. The moment was quickly replaced by suspicion and doubt. Why would he make an offer like that? What was his angle? Had he seen through the aggressive facade? Was he stringing me along only to renege at a later date? On a whim I decided to take a chance.

"You got a deal."

Janell told me later that Lenny had mad respect for me because I'd made it on my own for so long. I decided not to disclose the financial details of our arrangement because somehow I just didn't think it would sit well with her.

Lenny was an extremely clever businessman and naturally talented when it came to hustling. According to Lenny, he started pimping the day he exited his mother's womb. His mother spoiled him rotten, and being the only boy, his four sisters treated him like a king. In high school, he had at least ten girls at his disposal at all times without even trying. These girls didn't hesitate to use any and everything to include clothes, money, jewelry and sex, to get his attention. All of the girls knew about each other, but it only made them work harder to keep his attention. After high school, Lenny went to Delaney University, a Historically Black College in Tennessee with hopes of getting a degree in business. Of course, his parents wanted him to go to an all-white school, but that was completely out of the question. His primary goal was to obtain a Bachelor of Science in Business and later an MBA. In the end, he successfully completed all of his educational goals. However, the Doctorate of Philosophy in Pimping would prove to be far more lucrative than the other degrees could ever be.

During his freshman year, Lenny was kind of low key. He stuck to the books and basically used the time to scope things out. Sophomore year was a different story. Girls started throwing themselves at him left and right and because he never promised any of them a damn thing, he was free to move around without a lot of drama. If one of his girls saw him with someone else, they played by the rules: never step to Lenny in public and never ask him questions about other girls. The unspoken policy was to simply take it up with the other girl at another time and another place.

It didn't take Lenny long to realize his situation at Delaney was almost identical to the one back in high school. Only this time, he looked at it from a business perspective. He met with five of his biggest fans, pitched his business plan and they bought it. Lenny became a bona fide pimp and the rest was history. On the weekends, he would drive the girls to Memphis, which was only a few hours away. He had connections with a really upscale night club where the girls picked up their "clients." He was a generous pimp even back then. He let the girls keep 60% of the profit and he had their backs. The girls obviously liked the money, but most importantly, they had Lenny's attention. He was an absolute genius when it came to making every girl feel special and this would turn out to be his greatest attribute. In spite of the complexity of the situation, he was really close to the girls he ran back in college and had managed to keep in touch with them over the years. He was actually the godfather to the son of one of his ex-associates. Her ex-pro football player husband had no idea that his beautiful wife had more miles on her than the Kansas City Railroad, but it was cool. For Lenny, what happened in the past could stay in the past.

After graduation, Lenny had enough money to stop pimping and concentrate his efforts on legitimate business opportunities. With his business degree in hand and a seemingly unlimited amount of startup money, he decided to stay in the service industry. He opened a few small businesses around campus, to include a beauty salon, a car detail service, and a janitorial company. The money was good, but it was too time consuming. He spent twelve to sixteen hours a-day collecting money and making sure everyone knew who was in charge. He learned early on that you couldn't expect anyone, even your best friend, to be honest when it came to money. After a few years on the grind and a small fortune to show for his hard work, Lenny was bored. His businesses were successful and the money was constant, but he wanted to do something different. On a whim, he sold everything and headed west for California to explore his options. However, a quick stop in Vegas for a few days of relaxation would turn out to be the best business decision he ever made. To this day, he still hasn't been to California. He knew a gold mine when he saw one.

When Lenny gave up pimping after college, he vowed to never get caught up in the game again, because in his opinion and the words of Too Short, *Pimping Ain't Easy*. According to Lenny, a good pimp had to be a father, mother, lover, and from time to time, a disciplinarian. The disciplinarian role was the one he hated most. He was raised to cherish and respect women. Above all, he was taught that a man should never put his hands on a woman, but these girls were nothing like the women he grew up around. At times, it seemed as if they simply didn't give a damn about themselves. In addition, their ability to comprehend even the simplest detail was rarely enhanced by anything other than violence. This particular concept had puzzled him for years.

It had been years since Lenny left Delaney but there was one particular girl that always stayed on his mind. Her name was Tiffany. She reminded him of a chocolate doll and that's the name that he gave her. She was from a small town in Alabama, but everyone thought she was an island girl. She had dark, dark skin and long curly hair, which she usually wore in a ponytail. Of all the girls he'd known, Tiffany was the only one he had ever considered settling down with.

It was freshman year, English 101. When she walked into the room everything (noise, laughter, and time) seemed to stop. Her beauty was just that breathtaking. For the first time in his life, or at least since junior high, Lenny's confidence was shaken. He didn't know how to approach her. By the time the class was finally dismissed, his heart was literally pounding and he was sure that those closest to him could hear it. As it turns out he wouldn't get a chance to talk to her that day, which was fortunate, because he would have made a complete fool of himself. When the class met two days later, he was more composed. His confidence shot to the roof when she selected the seat directly in front of him. To his surprise, Tiffany made the first move. When class was over, she simply handed him a sheet of paper with her number and a message scrawled on it. To Lenny the message contained two of the most seductive words in the English language, "call me". They flirted for a few weeks and eventually started studying together. She was playing the coy game at first but he already knew the end result. When they finally made love Lenny discovered she was a virgin, a fact that she kept hidden until the last possible moment. He knew she was special from the second that he laid eyes on her, but this sealed it for him. For the first time in his life, Lenny was falling in love.

Tiffany became his world. She was the first thing on his mind when he woke up and the last thing on his mind when he went to sleep. But love was a strange emotion and one that Lenny was totally unfamiliar. However, he quickly learned that love could make you think and do crazy things. Whenever Tiffany wasn't in her dorm or she failed to answer her phone, he became a mad man. At first, he attributed his new feelings and behavior to jealousy. He knew the upper class guys were constantly hounding Tiffany and it drove him crazy. By mid-semester he knew that he was in love. He hid it for as long as he could but everything changed one rainy night in November. The semester was almost over and they were trying to spend as much time together as they could before going home for the winter break. Tiffany was lying in his arms when all of a sudden she started crying.

"Baby, what's wrong?" he asked, thinking that he had done something to upset her.

"I think I'm pregnant," Tiffany sobbed uncontrollably.

"What? I thought you were on the pill," Lenny said, in complete disbelief.

"I was, but they made me sick and I was gaining too much weight."

"How late are you?"

"Two weeks."

"Tiffany, if you're two weeks late then you're pregnant. Stop trying to wish it away," Lenny said thinking to himself this couldn't be happening.

"What the hell are we gonna do, Lenny?"

Without hesitating he said, "We'll have the baby. I'll get a job and we can move off campus next semester."

"But what about my parents?"

"Baby, don't worry I'll handle it. I'll talk to your family myself and I'll let your father know I'm an honorable man".

As grim as the situation seemed, Lenny was starting to get excited, a son and Tiffany with him all the time, what could be better?

"Tiffany," Lenny's voice was hoarse with emotion as he cradled her head between his hands, "I love you."

Words never formed by his lips to any woman except his mother rolled from his lips with ease.

Tiffany went home for the Christmas break while Lenny stayed around to find a job and a place for them to live. They talked every day but he noticed that while some days she sounded happy, most of the time he could hear something in her voice that frightened the living hell out of him.

A week before school started, he moved into the apartment and worked as much over time as he could. He was a ball of nerves the day before Tiffany was due to arrive.

"I'll be there on the four thirty bus, please be there on time," she told him the night before she left home.

He was there at four thirty as promised. The first thing he noticed when she got off the bus was her outfit: tight ass jeans and a tight ass sweater.

"Tiffany, you might as well stop trying to hide the fact that you're pregnant. You're gonna squeeze his brains out with that outfit you got on."

Tiffany kept walking toward the car as if she hadn't heard him.

"You hear me talking to you Tiffany? I'm sorry for yelling but I'm just concerned about the baby's health. I got some information on the clinic downtown. They will do the prenatal visits for cash so we won't have to worry about insurance. When you go into labor, we'll go to the nearest hospital. In other words, have the baby and worry about paying later."

"Lenny, I had an abortion."

"You did what!? How could you do something like that without talking to me?" Lenny yelled as his face turned crimson.

"For God's sake, Tiffany, I'm the father. I should have had a say in this too!"

For a few moments there was silence.

"I just couldn't do it. I couldn't tell my parents I was pregnant, so I took the money that you sent me..."

"The money that I sent you? You used the money that I sent you to kill my baby!"

He was only a few inches away from her face with the back of his hand but he stopped.

"Get out," he said quietly.

"But Lenny where am I gonna go? I gave up my room on campus."

"Tiffany, get out of my car. I can't stand to even look at you or smell you or hear your voice. As of right now, you don't exist!"

And that was the end of their relationship. She tried to persuade him to come back but he couldn't. She was tainted. To make matters worse he began hearing rumors about her dancing at one of the clubs in Memphis. Apparently, it was on the opposite side of town from his place of business. He considered checking it out for himself but decided he would rather not know the truth. The last time he saw her she was doing the sorority girl thing on campus. By then, Lenny had mastered the pimping game. Keeping up with his school-work and staying on top of his "business operations", allowed him to keep his mind free of Tiffany. One of his boys ran into her on campus shortly after Lenny graduated. She asked the guy to tell Lenny she'd gotten her life together and was planning to join the Army after graduation. In spite of the way things turned out, he was happy for her. Without a doubt, she was the only woman he ever loved. Ironically, she was also the catalyst to his successful career. Had things worked out between them, his career path would have been totally different. He often wondered if she knew the depth of the pain that she caused him. Did she know how much he really loved her?

Chapter Three

Latrice

I was getting really tired of Sierra and her never-ending drama, AND I was tired of my family always digging up the past. Why couldn't they just let it go? I think Sierra's biggest mistake was waiting until she was grown to tell them about Keith. The damage was already done and no one cared enough to do anything about it anyway.

Thankfully, I wasn't around the day Sierra finally snapped and spilled her guts but my aunt called later that night to find out if Keith had ever messed with me. Without hesitating, I said no and apparently Alex denied it as well. I never knew why Alex lied but for me it was simple. I didn't think anyone would believe me. Years later, when Sierra asked me why I didn't tell the truth, I explained my theory, "because of our silence, we are responsible for everything that happened to us."

Taking it a step further, I was older. Therefore, I should have done more to protect Sierra and Alex. I didn't include that part in my response to Sierra, but over the years, my guilt seemed to multiply on a daily basis. I often wondered how our lives might have been if I had done the right thing when we were kids.

Of course, the denial from Alex and me completely shattered Sierra's credibility, and from the moment of her confession, the family began to look at her differently. No one trusted her around their men and they accused her of every Tom, Dick and Harry in town. Almost immediately, she went from being a victim to being shunned by the entire family but no one really said anything to Keith. Her long overdue confession marked the beginning of the prolonged isolation period for Sierra. Eventually, she just left it all behind.

As much as I sympathized with Sierra, and in spite of my guilt, I had enough problems of my own. At twenty-one, I had a baby, a crack head for a husband and a habit of my own. My husband Jimmy was a decent man when I met him. He smoked a little weed from time to time, but that was it. Then, he met me and fell in love so damn fast it made my head spin. The good thing was he had a job and a house that his folks had given him. The bad thing was his inability to accept me along with all of my flaws. Before we got married, he constantly complained about me hitting the pipe. After the wedding, his complaining got worse. He worked all day and I got high all day. Eventually, he got tired of me spending all of his money and irritated with my unwillingness to quit using. His solution was to cut me off with the funds.

I tried many times to describe how I felt when I was high but he just didn't get it. One night I got a brilliant idea. I rolled a fat joint and laced it with a few rocks. After one hit of the primo, he was gone. The constant nagging became a thing of the past. Our primary focus in life at that point was getting high. But then I got pregnant and couldn't hit the pipe anymore. Well, not quite as often. It really pissed me off to see him enjoying it without me. As a matter of fact, he enjoyed it so much that he lost his job during my last month of pregnancy.   When J.T. came into the world, he had all the cards stacked against him. I look at him now and wonder why anyone would bring a child into such turmoil. But Jimmy wanted a son so I figured it was the least I could do considering the circumstances. We never really had time for J.T. and for some reason J.T. seemed to understand. Unlike most newborn babies, J.T. slept through the night from day one. After sleeping all night, he was content in his crib or playpen during the day requiring nothing but a bottle and a diaper change. Hell sometimes Jimmy and I would leave him in the middle of the night to locate Skeeter, our local dealer. We'd come back home hours later and find J.T. still asleep. I couldn't believe what a good baby we had.

Eventually, one of our neighbors reported us to child protection services for leaving J.T. at home alone and my mom took him for good. The day she came to get J.T. and his stuff, I was so high I couldn't remember her taking him. I woke up before Jimmy did that morning and found J.T.'s crib empty. I started screaming as loud as I could, finally waking Jimmy up. He was as confused as I was and just as distraught. We looked all over the house but J.T. was nowhere to be found. All of a sudden I was really sober. That was when I lost it for real. We went door to door looking for J.T. in our neighborhood.

"Mrs. Johnson I can't find J.T. He was in his crib when we went to bed and now he's gone!"

She peeped from behind her door and shaking her head.

"Latrice, you really need to get off that stuff."

At this point, I was shaking and sobbing and snot was flying everywhere.

"Mrs. Johnson, that ain't got nothing to do with this. Somebody came into my house and took my baby!"

Turns out Mrs. Johnson already knew the deal. She had watched my mom leave with J.T. and all of his stuff the previous night.

"Girl, why don't you go home and call your mother?"

"First of all, quit calling me girl. Second of all, we ain't got no phone! And what am I calling her for, she can't help us!"

"Latrice, just go on over to your mother's house and see what she has to say."

Mrs. Johnson always had a way of making me feel really small. On the rare occasion that the two of us engaged in conversation, she spoke to me as if I was a child. Her self-righteous behavior made me sick to my stomach. She thought she had the perfect family, perfect husband, and a perfect life. I wanted to tell her right then and there how many times a week I ran into Mr. Johnson at the crack house and just how many women he really had. Hell, even I gave it up to him for a couple of bumps on his pipe back when Jimmy and I first got married.

In the early days, I tried to make sure I had a few dollars before Jimmy left for work however, it didn't always work out that way. On one of those particular days, I was in need of a fix really bad and Jimmy wasn't due home for a few hours. I decided to try my luck and hit Mr. Johnson up for a couple of dollars. He came home for lunch a few days out of the week, but I couldn't remember which particular days. So I went outside around noon and just waited. Mrs. Johnson wasn't home, so when he drove up, I motioned for him to meet me at the corner of the house. He stopped me in the middle of my made up story about needing diapers for J.T. He reached into his jacket for a wallet I assumed, when out of his pocket fell a beautiful stone.

"You want some of this, Latrice?"

Of course I did, but I was totally shocked. Did he know how much the huge rock was worth? Without thinking twice, I agreed to some afternoon fun in exchange for the large gem. Mrs. Johnson wasn't home and I wasn't expecting Jimmy for at least a couple of hours. We went into my house and Mr. Johnson excused himself to the bathroom. I closed my eyes for a second and thought about the size of the rock that Mr. Johnson was carrying around. What was that all about? I opened my eyes to find Mr. Johnson with a lighter in one hand and the beautiful pipe in the other. I was immediately turned on. He lit up and hit the pipe like his middle name was Pookie from *New Jack City.* Up until that moment, I had no Idea that Mr. Johnson was a local rock star--not Mr. VP at the BMW dealership. Just the sight of his lips on the glass pipe was all the motivation I needed. What was a girl to do? After what took place that day, if I were Catholic, I'd have to say a thousand Hail Mary's to make things right.

Jimmy and I decided to walk the few blocks over to my mother's house to break the news about J.T. We both looked a mess. My weave was about two months overdue for touch-up and I had dried up snot all over my face. Jimmy was just as messed up as I was minus the bad weave. How was I going to tell my mother that J.T. was missing? Damn, I never should have let Jimmy talk me into trying that new concoction he came home with the night before. Supposedly, it was codeine pills mixed with Boone's Farm and cough syrup. After doing four glasses of it, I was in a coma.

"Take a deep breath, Latrice, and think about what we're gonna say," Jimmy said when we approached the front door.

But I couldn't come up with anything that made sense. I looked at Jimmy and got mad as hell. As the man of the house, wasn't he supposed to protect his family? I turned around and pounded on the door out of anger until my mom swung the door open.

"Momma, we woke up this morning and J.T. was gone. We don't know what happened to him," I sobbed uncontrollably. The look on her face said it all: disgust, hurt and concern, mixed with anger. I felt about two feet tall when I saw J.T. sitting at the kitchen table.

After that episode, Jimmy was even more determined to quit using. I was like, Negro please. Have you ever seen an ex-rock head around here? Hell no. You know why? Cause don't nothing get you off these rocks except death. The average lifespan of a person with a habit like ours is forty or fifty years old. If the dope didn't take you out, then something else would. Look at Mr. Ennis down the street. Everyone thought he had it all together and was just a casual user. A casual user my ass! He lost his house, his kids, both Benzes' and finally his life, messing around with Skeeter's money. He was one of those high and mighty, intellectual crack heads, trying to buck the system and get over on Skeeter. For some reason, he thought he could continue walking the streets owing Skeeter over two thousand dollars. On top of that, he threatened to blow the whistle on Skeeter's operation. A bullet between the eyes took care of that. He was 46 years old.

But Jimmy was still obsessed with the rehab thing and trying to get clean for J.T. He'd go in for thirty days and come home free from his addiction, with a new lease on life. Within thirty minutes, we would be hitting the pipe together. At first, I was a little disappointed with him for giving in so easily and I did what I could to support his fleeting sobriety. Eventually, I just had it waiting for him when he came home. Besides, I have a theory. Trying to get clean when you're not totally committed to the process is the craziest thing a rock head could ever do. Take my brother Donald, for example. He managed to stop using for about three months. He even moved up town and stopped hanging out with us. I was beginning to think he was really gonna make it. I was proud of him and prayed that he would stay clean. Hell, I figured if he could do it then maybe there was still hope for me.

Turns out that it was only wishful thinking. One day, he came to my mom's house with that unmistakable look on his face. It was a look that I knew all too well. He also had the nervous twitch, which was a tell-tale sign of a true rock star. I knew he wanted to get high but I immediately tried to talk him out of it. It was useless. On top of that, he had a pocket full of money and I was broke as hell.

I had an uneasy feeling when I hopped into his car and headed over to one of our most dependable spots for scoring. Porche, the chick who ran the spot was skinny as a rail and looked like walking death. Anyone would assume she was her own best customer, but no one ever saw her actually hit the pipe.

As we made our way up the gravel point road, I felt obligated to try one last time.

"Donald, it's been three months. Are you sure this is what you wanna do?"

"Yep, I'm sure. I gave it my best shot. For some reason I just can't seem to shake back. I'm a crack-head. Guess I'll be one until the day I die".

As we walked up the rickety old steps, Porche met us at the door with a sly look on her face.

"What the hell you doing over here Donald? Word on the street you supposed to be clean," she said through the two remaining teeth in her mouth.

"That's none of your damn business Porche," I said quickly, noticing the look of shame across my brother's face. "Just go in the house and come back with some good shit. An eight ball if you have one."

"No need to get fresh with me Latrice--I'm just saying. Donald ain't been 'round here for a minute. Thought he was gonna be one of the ones to get that monkey off his back for good".

She turned around and went into the house and came back with one of the fattest eight balls I'd ever seen. I'm sure she saw the excitement in my eyes.

"Just for you Donald. That's the purest shit you ever gonna get your hands on," she bragged and handed over the plastic baggie.

"Enjoy."

Before Donald could give her the hundred and fifty dollars, I inspected the merchandise. The going price for an ounce of rock cocaine was anywhere from five to eight hundred dollars. An eighth of an ounce was about a hundred to one-fifty depending on the purity. Like a professional jeweler, I looked for color and clarity. The sandy, yellowish-brown appearance of the gem told me all I needed to know.

"Pay her. She's right. This is the purest I've ever seen."

We took a few hits before pulling out of her drive way and headed back to my mom's.

We sat outside and quietly passed the pipe like old times. The beautiful gem was gone in less than an hour. We ended up making three or four more trips to Porsche's that night and I completely lost count of the number of rocks we smoked. We just kept going until Donald's pockets were completely empty. On our last trip to Porsche's, I remember her saying something about Donald spending over a grand and that she was completely out.

Soaring in my own world of pleasure and higher than even I could ever imagine, I wasn't really paying attention to Donald. He was hitting the pipe just as hard as I was and I forgot to remind him that it was his first ride in three months.

After finishing off the last rock we parted ways. Donald went into the house and I took a stroll up the street to see if anyone else was in the sharing mood. A few hours later I walked into my mother's house just as all hell was breaking loose. Donald was lying on the living room floor barely conscious and my mom was on the phone shouting at the 911 dispatcher,

"What's taking so long?! My son is dying, we need help now?!"

A few seconds later the paramedics arrived. By this time, I was kneeling on the floor with Donald's head in my lap.

"Dee, you can't do this. It ain't supposed to go down like this. Please say something."

He opened his eyes one last time and tried to speak, "Latrice.... I," and that was it. The paramedics hooked him up to the monitors and after a brief moment announced that he was in cardiac arrest. They placed him on the stretcher and rushed him out of the house.

My mother was hysterical and my dad stood motionless at the door as the paramedics rushed to the nearest hospital. Somehow I managed to get everyone into the car and I, of all people was the only one capable of driving us to the hospital.

When we arrived, Alex and my aunt Mae were already standing in the lobby. My grandmother, Aunt Birdie and Sierra arrived shortly after. We sat in the waiting room quietly praying and anxiously awaiting someone to come out and tell us what we already knew. He was gone before he left the house. In my heart, I knew he died in my arms.

After what seemed like an eternity, the doctor finally emerged from behind the double doors. My mom lost it before he said the words I'll never forget,

"We tried our best but we couldn't get him back..."

The remainder of his words were lost in the horrible sounds of pain and despair.

"...if anyone would like to view the remains come with me. We've already contacted the coroner and he'll be here any moment. Because of his age, there will be a mandatory autopsy...."

I couldn't listen anymore. As I ran for the nearest door, I noticed Alex was the only one to follow the doctor into the next room. Once outside I fell to my knees and begged God to take me. It should have been me in the first place. And then, I became angry--angry with God and angry with myself. But most of all, I was angry with Porche. This was all her fault. Why would she knowingly sell us the purest stuff she had when Donald was three months clean? I couldn't wait to get my hands on her. Then, there was guilt. I failed him. It was like placing a gun to his head and pulling the trigger. I never should have let him smoke so much.

And that's why I ain't stopping until St. Peter comes down from heaven and tells me that I'm going to make it. Jimmie can do whatever the hell he wants to do.

Chapter Four

Alex

When I was a junior in college, I applied for an Army ROTC scholarship and got it. I wanted to see the world and in addition, I had my eye on the fifty thousand dollar incentive for three years of service. I was planning to use the money for law school. I graduated on schedule with a 3.75 grade point average and a degree in political science and English. My family was proud of course, but they couldn't understand why I wanted to join the Army. As a Vietnam veteran and extremely reluctant draftee my father respected the military, but he never encouraged any of us to join. However, after he saw me on stage in my military uniform and the shiny gold bars on my shoulders, he finally gave me his approval and sent me on my way.

Two weeks after graduation, I was in Colorado on my first assignment. There were about three hundred brand new Second Lieutenants in my group. After signing in, we had three days to in-process and find out what the hell was going on. There were a few cuties in my class and things were looking good for me in the relationship department. With three males to every female, the odds of finding my future husband were definitely in my favor.

Day number three of in-processing put a damper on all of my aspirations concerning relationships. We were instructed to report to the troop medical center for a comprehensive physical exam, which included HIV testing. I had contemplated being tested many times before but fear caused me to change my mind every time. This time, I didn't have a choice.

A few days after the testing, we got a summons for an impromptu formation and no details were given about the purpose of the meeting. This was it. The results from the tests were in, I thought, and took a deep breath. Rumors were spreading as we made our way to the designated area. My classmates were convinced that the formation was called to discuss the issue of positive drug screenings. Apparently, it was customary to lose at least one soldier per class due to the Army's stringent drug abuse policy. Once we were all assembled, the commander wasted no time.

"Group, Atten-n-n-tion. Come forward when your name is called".

Our lab results were in. I almost fainted. When they called my name I went to the front of the classroom and retrieved the little white envelope. Once all of the envelopes were distributed, we were dismissed. I headed straight for the bathroom and locked myself in a stall. Another girl was right behind me. My hands were shaking to the point that I could barely open the envelope. I was negative. I started crying and making all kind of promises to the Lord. When I finally emerged from the stall, I immediately noticed the other girl. Her name was Tiffany. She was crying too, but they weren't tears of joy. Her test was positive. She was instructed to report to the clinic for a more sensitive test. According to her, there was no need for further testing. She was devastated, but she said she wasn't surprised. She believed the disease was God's way of punishing her, "for her multitude of sins" as she described it.

In between sobs she kept saying something about this guy named Lenny, but I couldn't really understand anything else she was saying. I didn't know what to do so we sat in the bathroom and cried until one of the platoon leaders came in looking for us. Tiffany just sat there in a trance. I came up with a story about Tiffany's grandmother being seriously ill "she needs to get home immediately," I told the manly looking lady who immediately sprang into action. Before we knew it, she had

Tiffany booked on a flight to Alabama on emergency leave. Tiffany thanked me for the quick lie and said she didn't want to face her ordeal with a bunch of strangers. She just wanted to get home and find a way to break the news to her family and some guy named Lenny.

The topic for the next day was a no brainer: sexually transmitted diseases and its prevalence in the military. At the end of the briefing we were informed that we had lost not just one, but three of our fellow classmates due to adverse administrative findings. You didn't need a degree in rocket science to figure this one out. Three of our classmates had tested positive for HIV, Tiffany wasn't the only one. The room was silent as everyone looked around in disbelief. No one could imagine how something like that could happen or what they would've done if it had happened to them.

I didn't hear from Tiffany after she left, even though I tried several times to get in touch with her by phone. I often found myself thinking about her, wondering if she was still alive, had she developed full blown AIDS, what did her family say or do? And who the hell was Lenny?

Needless to say, that particular experience made a real impact on my life, for a while anyway. After the Tiffany situation I vowed to never put myself at risk again, but with all the cuties running around, it was hard to stay focused. To keep myself out of the realm of temptation, I spent most of my time in my room. When I got tired of studying I'd read a book or watch CNN. As a matter of fact, that's what I was doing when I heard about Tupac. I was in a state of shock and disbelief. Tupac was a genius in my opinion and his greatest hits compilation is a permanent fixture in my CD changer to this day.

I managed to stay out of trouble for a while, but all of that changed, when I had to call one of my instructors in reference to a homework assignment. When we got the homework issue resolved, Major Smiley got kind of personal. Where was I from? Why didn't I hang out with my classmates?

"I bet you got a man back home, don't you?" he commented.

After carefully choosing my words my response was, "No, I don't have a man back home or anywhere else for that matter, sir."

"Sir?" he chuckled on the other end of the phone at my futile attempt to preserve some professionalism in our conversation.

"And why not, Alexandra?" he said.

The way he said my name caused my heart to skip a beat. When I failed to respond, he chuckled again.

He continued with his not so subtle attempt to break through the wall that surrounded me. Major Smiley couldn't have known how good I was at playing the game he was trying to play and my plan was to keep it that way. I was determined to stay out of trouble. I decided to keep quiet for a moment to see exactly where he was going with the conversation. At the same time, I was flattered by the attention. The brother was fine as hell.

"You are without a doubt, one of the most attractive sisters to ever come through my class, and you mean to tell me you don't have a man? What's up with that?"

At that point, I figured I might as well cut the crap and give him the real reason I was being low key.

"With all due respect, sir, I guess I'm just trying to stay away from all the extra drama I see going on around here. Everyone is in player mode. I had my share of that in college."

This time, the sexy little chuckle was replaced by a boisterous laugh.

"Wait," he said and tried to control his laughter, "HBCU, right?"

"Yes," I said ready to pounce at the first sign of ridicule for my having attended a Black college. I had already met a couple of other Black officers who turned their noses up when I told them where I had gone to school. For some reason, these individuals felt they were superior because they received their commissions from White universities. The crab theory was alive and well even in the U.S. Army. Not knowing much about the Major on the other end of the phone, there was a possibility that he felt the same way.

"What about you?" I asked with just a tinge of attitude in my voice.

"Mississippi Valley State. SWAC all the way!"

"Are you serious?" I asked feeling somewhat embarrassed by my stereotypical assumption.

"In that case, we're family. We kicked y'all's ass every year I was in school."

"Ok, you're from Louisiana so let me guess, Gretna or Southwestern?"

"Black and gold," I said, not hiding my surprise over the fact that he even had to ask.

We ended up talking for hours reminiscing on our college days. For the first time since graduation, it finally dawned on me that those days were gone forever. Regardless of all the mistakes and bad decisions I made during those years, the good times far outweighed the bad.

We finally ended the conversation with Major Smiley asking me out to dinner the next night. I politely declined, using the upcoming exam as my excuse.

"You know I have to do well to represent the SWAC," I said, letting him know I was hip to the fact that officers from HBCU's were not expected to perform as well as officers who attended White colleges. No way was I going to become a part of that dialogue.

"Cool, I understand completely. By the way I really enjoyed our conversation and from the looks of it Gretna is doing a damn good job with their ROTC program. Good luck on your test, maybe we can go out and celebrate afterwards."

Just when I was about to respond, he cut me off with a quick, "Good night Alex. I will talk to you soon," then he was gone.

My mind was all over the place. Not only was he fine as hell, he was also intelligent and funny with just the right amount of rough neck in him to make me almost forget about the promise I made to myself. I just couldn't get him out of my mind. Stunning. That was the only thing that came to mind when I pictured him in his starched camouflage uniform, which looked like they were tailor made just for him. His eyes were light brown, not hazel, but just light enough to provide the perfect contrast against his chocolate skin. Damn! I had only one month left in Colorado before heading to North Carolina for my permanent assignment and here I was fantasizing about one of my instructors. That night I prayed for the strength that I knew I was going to need in order to resist this temptation.

The next morning I decided on a plan of action--I would just avoid him. My plan worked. But as much as I didn't want to admit it, I was disappointed when he didn't call me that night. Maybe he found another brand new second lieutenant to kick it with for the next few weeks.

That night I prayed again, "Thank you God for giving me the strength to resist this temptation. Amen."

On Wednesday, the day of our big test, I got up extra early. I put a lot of effort into my hair and make-up. There was not very much I could do about my outfit, army fatigues were definitely the wardrobe for the day. I knew I would run in to Major Smiley at some point during the day. Although I was in the process of resisting temptation, I saw nothing wrong with trying to look nice. I also decided to at least make a point to say hello if I saw him. I made it to the class room a few minutes early, however, I chose to take a seat in the back because I like to know what's going on around me at all times. By my estimation, I expected to run into Major Smiley after the test. To my surprise, he walked into the classroom and proceeded to tell us that he was the proctor for the exam. Once again, Major Smiley made my heart skip a beat. On top of that, I had this extremely familiar feeling in the pit of my stomach. He was even sexier than I thought. His sleeves were rolled up exposing the brand I knew all too well. Surprisingly, he failed to mention his fraternity affiliation. He was a Que Dog. My mind immediately traveled back to my first day at Gretna, when my ghetto roommate and I innocently walked by Q-Hill and ended up at a "house party" with only four attendees. As scandalous as it was, that night would become one of my most memorable experiences at Gretna. And even more scandalous is the fact that I am still a sucker for a Q.

I was impressed by the fact that he omitted the information about his fraternity affiliation during our lengthy telephone conversation. Most of the guys in the class, along with some of the instructors, couldn't wait to divulge such information because it was necessary to elevate their game. And the sisters were no different, paraphernalia head to toe every chance they got. But not me, I brought one pink and green t-shirt and I slept in it most of the time. I love my sorority and knew at the age of five the direction I would take. However, I didn't want to be defined exclusively by one affiliation. I usually allow people to discover my association on their own. Apparently, Major Smiley lived by the same code. This was definitely a plus.

Major Smiley started handing out the tests and giving out administrative information. When he reached my desk, he hesitated for a split second and gazed into my eyes. I had to admit, it was extremely hard for me to maintain my military bearing, but somehow I managed. He handed me the test and said, "Good luck class," without ever taking his eyes off of me.

I went through the test as calmly as I could. But when I got to the end I found myself looking at the answer key. I was in complete shock but the little gift couldn't have come at a better time. The test was in my worst subject and I was sure I'd bombed it. First, I looked around to see who was left in the class. When I finally had enough courage, I looked over at Major Smiley. He seemed to be completely oblivious to what was going on. I went through the test again feeling guilty about my stroke of luck, but changing two of my answers which had been wrong. Suddenly, there were only five people left in the room including myself and the major. I looked over at him again and this time he was smiling. That was a gangster move. I turned my test in with a sticky note attached to it. "Call me," the note said and at precisely six pm that night my phone rang.

"Congratulations Lieutenant, you aced the test. However, I am compelled to let you know I noticed only two of your answers were changed. You would have done just fine without my help."

"Thank you, Major Smiley. I appreciate your kindness and I would love to go out and celebrate with you, if the invitation is still there of course."

We went to dinner and then to a little park on the other side of town. After struggling with all of the events that had taken place that day and trying to keep the conversation as bland as possible for as long as we could, he finally kissed me. All of my inhibitions were gone, just like that. On the way back, I watched him as he carefully maneuvered his way through the busy traffic. I tried to figure out how the experience which had taken place only moments before could be so beautiful, when we barely knew each other. As we turned into the gate leading to the base, I silently asked God to forgive me. This was nothing new, I always asked for forgiveness whenever I gave in to the sins of the flesh, but this time was different. For some reason, I felt worse than I'd ever felt before. When Major Smiley dropped me off, he kissed me in the palm of my hand and said, "I will call you tomorrow".

I ran to my room took a shower, replaying the events of the evening over and over in my mind. As I fell asleep, I had the urge to call him. I just wanted to hear his voice, but I realized I only had the number to his office.

Regardless of the fact that we were breaking a number of military rules, we still kicked it whenever we could. I finally got around to asking him about the test. I wanted to know if he did it because he felt I was incapable of doing well on my own. According to him, he never doubted my ability to do well. He said he did it because I was so stressed out about the test. He just wanted to make sure I was ok. He put the answer key at the end of the test in hopes that I wouldn't look ahead and find it. In the end it worked out just as he planned and he was proud of me. His response made me feel a little better. I definitely didn't want him to think I was an idiot.

As always, I fell hard and I fell fast. Before I knew it I was in love. With just a few weeks remaining in the course, the time seemed to accelerate just when I was starting to have some fun.

On the night of our hail and farewell ball, I discovered the origin of that sinking feeling I had on our first date. According to protocol all of the instructors were required to bring their spouses. For some reason, I had never gotten around to discussing Smiley's marital status. He didn't wear a ring so I just assumed he was single. After counting the number of males and females at the head table a few times, my assumption appeared to be correct. He was most definitely a bachelor. It wasn't until the end of the ceremony when I discovered the truth. During his final toast, the general congratulated Major Smiley on the birth of his baby girl, who was five weeks old. My mouth literally fell open as Major Smiley immediately looked over at me with this weird expression on his face. Time stood still as I struggled to conceal my emotions. As soon as I thought I was able to walk, I excused myself from the table pretending to be nauseated from all of the wine I had consumed.

"I feel sick. I'm going to the bathroom to make myself throw up," I told the girl sitting next to me.

"You want me to go with you," she said with genuine concern.

"No, I'll be ok. I think I just had one to many."

When I reached the bathroom, I threw up without even trying and it wasn't because of the wine. I threw up out of disgust. How could I have been so stupid? There were signs everywhere. All I had was a pager and cell phone number. All of our dates were strategically planned to take place when he was assigned to twenty-four hour duty. And we never went to his place, "a lot of the staff members live on my street," he said when I asked him about hanging out at his place. I bought it-- hook, line and sinker. Either this guy was good or I was just plain stupid. I took a long hard look in the mirror and though out loud, "here I go again."

I couldn't leave the party yet because there were still some awards to be presented. Not that I thought I was getting one or anything, it was just customary to stay until all of the awards were presented. I had to sit there for another hour trying to laugh at the corny jokes as I fought to hold back the tears.

"Lieutenant Alexandra Phillips, please come forward," General Brookins said. I received a sharp elbow from the girl next to me when I failed to respond. My mind was a million miles away. Somehow I made it to the podium, which was situated just a few feet away from Smiley. With all of the dignity I could muster, I managed to stand at attention for the presentation.

"For outstanding performance in both academics and leadership, Lieutenant Phillips is receiving our two most prestigious awards: The Golden Eagle and the Junior Leadership Award. Congratulations Lieutenant," he said as he shook my hand and presented me with a plaque and a coin from his personal collection.

He went on to explain the significance of the achievement. Apparently, since the induction of the two awards over thirty-five years ago, only five other students had the privilege of receiving both awards simultaneously. One of those individuals happened to be General Benjamin Roundtree, a retired two star general and graduate of Gretna, my alma mater. I was in absolute shock. I knew I was doing well academically and getting good scores in our leadership assignments but I had no idea that I was doing that well. The academic award was obviously based on grade point average. Just when I was starting to wonder if Major Smiley had somehow influenced the leadership award, General Brookins described the selection process. Votes for the Junior Leadership award were cast in a private ballot and none of the staff members were aware of the outcome until that night.

"By the way," General Brookins continued, "Lieutenant Phillips is the first female recipient of the leadership award. Congratulations." When the picture taking and cheers were over, I had to shake hands with members of the staff. When it was time to shake hands with Major Smiley, I felt faint. It was actually the grip of his handshake that kept me on my feet. Hopefully, no one else noticed.

When I finally made it back to my seat, my friend, Keesha, whispered.

"Girl, I guess you really were studying all the damn time. We all thought you had some other stuff going on and just wanted to keep it on the D. L."

I managed to smile but all I could think about was getting the hell out of Colorado. Even though I had seven days to report to my next duty station, I planned to be packed and ready to leave as soon as the graduation ceremony was over. Until then, I was going to avoid Major Smiley by any means necessary. In spite of my efforts, our paths crossed the day before graduation at the post office of all places. We were in uniform so I had to maintain my cool. After all, it was against the rules for a junior officer to use profanity when interacting with a senior officer. However, I got my point across by taking a painfully civil approach. I listened to his sob story about not being happy at home, his numerous efforts to tell me he was married, and the proverbial "just couldn't find the right words." Basically, he said all of the things I expected him to say, but when I looked into his eyes I saw the sincerity. Was it even possible? He gave me a piece of paper with the name of a hotel and room number.

"I'll be there tonight at six. I have so many things to say to you before you leave Alex," he said softly.

I turned my back to walk away knowing that in such a public place there was little that he could do to physically stop me. Instead he stopped me with his words.

"Please, Alex. Your graduation is tomorrow. I've got to see you before you leave."

As I took the slip of paper from his hands, I wondered if I could find the strength to stay in my room that night. At ten minutes to six, I was in my car. As I made my way to the hotel, I decided it was probably a good idea to hear what he had to say. Perhaps it would accelerate the healing process. At six fifteen, I was standing outside of room one twenty one thinking about all of the reasons I should simply turn and walk away. I was weak for this man. Being there was a huge mistake, but just as I turned to leave, he opened the door.

"Hi Alex. I was just about to go downstairs to wait for you," he said with a half-smile.

"This is a mistake. I need to leave." I told him apologetically.

"Leave? Why?" he asked appearing to be completely clueless as to why I would want to do such a thing.

"Because this is wrong and I shouldn't be here," I said feeling the lump form in my throat as the tears rolled down my face.

He grabbed my hand and pulled me inside. The hotel suite was huge, with a king sized bed and adjoining kitchenette. In one corner, there were six vases filled with pink roses and each bouquet had a little note. In the other corner was a table with a bottle of my favorite wine and yet another note. Next to it was my favorite scented candle, "Shea Culture". It was made by a local retailer which I discovered during an outing with Major Smiley. On the bed I found pink rose petals and a rectangular box. As I walked around the room and collected each note, he stood in the doorway of the bedroom and nervously analyzed my every move. I noticed he was wearing the royal blue silk pajamas that I purchased for him on his birthday.

My speech was planned. I was going to tell him what a sorry excuse for a man he was, how disrespectful he'd been to his wife and to me, and how I hoped to never see him again. But I couldn't get any of those words out. I was barely breathing. When he held out his hand, I took it. For a moment, he just stared into my eyes, but when his glare became too intense, I turned away. He quickly turned my face back toward him and began to kiss me with such passion that I felt my knees buckle. He removed my shirt and kissed every inch of my torso igniting a fire within my body that was sure to explode if he continued. We made love continuously that night and each time I fell asleep, I was awakened by a kiss or a touch that started the process all over again. By daybreak, I was totally spent. What took place the night before was absolutely beautiful, but I couldn't forget the fact that he was a married man. And then, the tears came. I couldn't help it. I loved this man with all of my heart and soul, but he would never be mine and I had to learn how to live without him. While he was still asleep, I took a quick shower and left as fast as I could. I didn't know how to say goodbye and I couldn't deal with the empty promises that were sure to come.

I made my escape immediately after the graduation ceremony. I made the seventeen hundred mile journey in record time, but it still felt like an eternity. I thought about Major Smiley during the entire trip and envisioned his reaction to waking up and finding me gone. Was he going to contact me? Did he really care about me or was I just another young officer to add to his long list of personal achievements?

Since I arrived two days early, I checked into a hotel just outside the base and planned to use the free time to relax and clear my head. That night, I finally opened the box that Smiley had given me. Inside was a beautiful heart shaped necklace encrusted with diamond and garnet stones. The note said,
Dear Alex,

You are forever a part of my life, my thoughts and my soul. I can barely breathe at the thought of never seeing you again. Wear this for me. I want to remain close to your heart. I love you Alex. I only wish you knew how much. If you ever need me, just call.

Always, Smiley

I guess time really does heal all wounds. Slowly, I came to terms with yet another painful experience. However, this

61

experience had the greatest impact on my attitude toward relationships and it truly set the tone for the rest of my time in the army. I met a few interesting guys but they never came close to my personal space. My guard was always up, but on a few rare occasions, curiosity almost got the best of me. However, a quick moment of reflection took care of that. Once again, a painful experience would become the motivating force in my life.

I became engrossed in my quest to become an attorney. By day, I was in charge of the administrative section of the hospital, answering directly to the hospital commander. The position would later influence my decision to specialize in medical malpractice. At night, I took review courses in hopes of getting a good score on the LSAT and getting accepted into law school. My plan paid off with huge dividends. My test score was high enough for me to compete and gain acceptance to the law school of my choice. I chose Georgetown University. My four years on active duty went by faster than I anticipated and I was a little ambivalent about resigning my commission, but that was the plan. Sticking to the plan was the one thing I'd always been good at. My military discharge became official just in time for me to start the fall semester.

Ironically, a week before my departure I met Lawrence, a drop dead gorgeous senior enlisted soldier who also worked in the hospital. He resembled a slightly smaller version of The Rock from *The Fast and the Furious*. I had seen him around a few times and remembered thinking, what the hell is he doing in the army? He should be modeling or making movies or something. He happened to be a light skinned brother, which was usually not my cup of tea. After talking to him, I got past the initial flaw and I discovered he was just a cool down to earth brother. For some reason, he appeared to be completely oblivious of the fact that he was the talk of the entire military installation.

We met at the gym, after I caught him checking *me* out in the mirror. I have to admit, I did find myself thinking of ways to introduce myself, but decided against it. As luck would have it or as a result of strategic planning on his part, we finished our workouts at the same time. While exiting the building, we reached for the same door handle. It turned out to be an excellent opportunity to strike up a conversation.

"Excuse me ma'am, do you work in the hospital?" he asked as we exited the building.

"Yes, I work in the admin section and you work in the orthopedics department, right?" I said with a smile.

I couldn't resist the urge to flirt just a little.

"Captain Phillips, my friends call me Alex," I said with a handshake.

"Sergeant Gardner. Please call me Lawrence, if you don't mind," he replied.

We stood in the parking lot and talked for a while before we agreed to go out that evening to the comedy club. It was military discount night. It seemed pretty harmless since I was leaving in a few days. I hadn't been out on a date since I left Colorado, so I was kind of nervous. We met at his apartment and to my surprise he had dinner waiting for me. With Al Green playing softly in the background, we ate tacos and drank a few strawberry margaritas until it was time to leave for the club. We learned a lot about each other in a short period of time. The conversation was effortless and purposeful as if we were trying to make up for lost time. He was divorced with two kids and an ex-wife who cheated on him. After giving her a second chance, she did it again. What the hell was her problem? I was literally dying to ask that question, but I didn't. I figured it was too soon to let him know exactly how much I was attracted to him. He expressed his desire to get married again but vowed to wait until he was retired. He blamed the frequent absences away from home for the destruction of his first marriage. Based on the number of years he'd already served, he was talking at least seven more years.

"Wow, seven years?" I asked trying not to show my disappointment.

"Would you change your mind if the right person came along?"

He gave me a devilish smile and proceeded to change the subject.

"Have you ever been married Alex?"

"No, I haven't."

"You gotta be kidding me. Why not?"

To my surprise, his curiosity seemed genuine. My answer to that question as always, "I haven't found the right person."

"What are you looking for, Alex?"

Again, his sincerity blew me away.

I hesitated for a moment in order to give the question some real thought for a change, not only for him but for myself as well.

"I don't know."

He grabbed my hand and smiled as we drove to the club. I only had a few days left before I would be leaving the army for good and starting law school. For the remainder of my time there, we were inseparable. That was the beginning of our long distance relationship. It lasted five years.

According to most of my friends, I had to be crazy to think that Lawrence could be faithful. First of all, he was drop-dead gorgeous and had charisma for days. He could have any woman he chose. I brought those issues to his attention on numerous occasions and he was adamant about the fact that he was a one-woman man, and I believed him. Even when he was transferred to Hawaii for two years, I still believed in our relationship. And since I was busy with law school, I didn't really have time to worry about it. I just looked forward to the times when we were together. I remember the day I dropped him off at the airport for his transfer to Hawaii.

He said, "Alex you don't have to worry about me and what I'm doing over there. We can make this work. I will never hurt you. As long as you hold up your end, I can do the same. Do you understand what I'm saying, Alex?"

Through the tears I managed to respond.

"I believe you Lawrence but do you know how many beautiful women…."

"I don't care how many beautiful women there are in Hawaii. I'm with the person that I want to be with. As long as you're faithful to me you will never have to worry about me being unfaithful to you."

I nodded while my silent tears turned into an uncontrollable sob.

"Alex, I need you to listen to me," he whispered and then repeated his last statement, "As long as you are faithful to me, you will never have to worry about me being unfaithful to you."

"But Lawrence…."

"No. Alex, I need you to listen and really understand what I'm saying to you. Do you love me?"

"Yes."

"Do you trust me?"

"Yes."

"Good, but I need you to hear me and hear me well. Temptation is a problem in most relationships, but it's an even bigger problem for us. The moment you give into temptation is the moment you'll lose your faith in our relationship. The same applies to me."

65

Chapter Five

Sierra

I wasn't sure how the Lenny thing was going to work. His generosity made me a little suspicious. There had to be some type of angle. I just didn't have time to figure it out with all the other drama that I had going on. I finally got to see some sunshine after two weeks of being cooped up in the hospital. I dreamt about hot bubble baths in a real tub but that could wait. The first thing I did was call home and as expected, my mother immediately started with her sermon.

"Sierra, two weeks is too long for us to go without hearing from you. We thought something horrible happened to you. Why won't you just come home? Are you going to church out there? You need to …"

"Momma, just let me talk to the kids because I can't handle the drama right now."

She put Damarcus, my oldest son on the phone first. It took less than two minutes for him to warm up and drop the attitude after I promised to send him some new Air Jordan's and the latest play station game. Tray, on the other hand, was a different story. At seven, he was clearly the more sensitive of the two and it usually required significantly more effort to appease him. Not only did I promise to send a new pair of kicks and the money for a new bike, I also promised to come home for Christmas which was less than four months away. As I agreed to the latter, I knew I would end up disappointing him once again. I hadn't been home for Christmas for a few years and was definitely not planning a trip for this year. I decided to just deal with his disappointment when the time came.

After ending the call with a quick hello to my grandmother, I wandered over to the mirror and for the first time, I took a long look at myself and the hideous scar that was permanently etched on my once perfect abs. I couldn't stand looking at it, but I realized that aside from the surgical scar there were no other signs of what really happened. With the bruises on my face finally faded enough to be concealed with make-up, I decided I still had it going on. I can't pose nude of course, but I was never in to that anyway. I decided that if anyone asked, I would tell them I had C-sections with both my kids. Aside from the physical scars, I had psychological issues to deal with. The nightmares were getting worse. Fear was an unacceptable emotion in this line of business. Yet another bridge I had to cross when I came to it.

When Janell picked me up from the hospital that morning, we went straight to her place where Lenny patiently awaited our arrival. From there, he planned to take me to my new place. We both agreed that I should take a few more weeks to rest before I went back to work. Because of my new employee status, Lenny's goal at this point was to lay the ground rules for employment in his organization. He sent Janell on an errand and immediately started to explain his rules of operation. The rules were pretty straightforward to say the least. Rule number one: Lenny decided when, where, how and with whom we conducted business. We worked certain days during the week and when we were off, we were instructed to stay away from the hot areas of town. That particular rule actually made sense because I had seen plenty of girls get busted because they'd become a familiar face. Familiar faces were always suspect in this town, so needless to say, I was definitely in agreement with rule number one. Rule number two: we were to have mandatory physicals every three months. If anyone came up hot, they were automatically terminated no questions asked. Lenny came up with that particular rule through years of experience. For some strange reason, some of his girls just refused to use condoms. No matter how many times he warned them about STD's, a few of them still tested positive for everything under the sun to include, gonorrhea, chlamydia, herpes and HIV.

Raquel was one of his main girls back at Delaney. Lenny implemented the quarterly testing rule after she tested positive for HIV. In order to ensure compliance, he insisted the rule was strictly in the interest of protecting his business and its reputation. In reality, he did it because he was one of the few pimps who actually gave a damn about the women who kept his pockets lined and also because of the guilt and anguish he felt when Raquel tested positive. Raquel was from Arkansas. She was somewhat pretty, but her body was definitely her greatest asset. She had an 18-inch waist with an ass like a pony. She was also a straight 'A' student with plans of becoming a social worker. Ironically, her long-term goal was to open a group home for wayward girls. She was one of the campus geeks during the week, but on the weekends the schoolgirl image disappeared along with her clothes. For Raquel, the sky was the limit when it came to material possession. As a result, she frequently took risks that proved to be fatal for her in the end. She tested positive for HIV during her senior year. After narrowing down the list of potential suspects, she came up with two names. She wanted revenge, but it didn't turn out that way. She received a life sentence for murder and attempted murder. Ironically, the guy that she fatally wounded didn't have the virus, the one who survived was positive.

Going to the clinic every three months and allowing Lenny to arrange my schedule was cool but the part about Lenny controlling what we did on our days off didn't sit well with me. What if I wanted to do a little free-lancing? I decided to play that one by ear. After all, Lenny wasn't omnipresent. There was no way for him to keep tabs on twenty girls all day, every day. The next rule was one that I really liked. We lived where Lenny wanted us to live and from the looks of Janell's place he didn't half step. I couldn't wait to get out of that rat hole I called home. I'd spent more than a few nights on the street just to get out of there.

After receiving my lecture from Lenny, we left Janell's and headed to my new place. As I expected, the place was absolutely beautiful. It was a tri-level two-bedroom apartment with a single car garage located just off the strip and it was fully furnished. Lenny had gone through the trouble of having me make a list of the things I wanted to keep from my old place. I noticed three large boxes stacked neatly on the table in the dining area. The rest was given to Goodwill.

After a total of six of weeks of convalescing, I was ready to go to work for Lenny. At the same time, I tried to figure out how to work my side gigs just in case he decided to back out of our deal. My first night out was a piece of cake. I got paid five hundred dollars to sit at a black jack table with an elderly high roller for two hours. My next date was a fifteen-minute gig, straight missionary with some silly white boy who wanted to see what it was like to do a sister. The cost for that one was two hundred and fifty dollars. That grand total was $750 for two hours and fifteen minutes of work and all I had to do was sit back and wait for Lenny to call me with the details for my next gig.

I sort of figured this man was not an ordinary pimp, but when I found out we had drivers to transport us to and from our appointments, I was convinced. I had finally made it to the big time and at the rate I was going, I figured I wouldn't need any side gigs. In all, I made two thousand dollars on my first night for four hours of work: twelve hundred for me and eight hundred for Lenny. I got up early the next day and went straight to the toy store to buy my kids some new play station games. From there, I went to the mall and bought each of them a pair of new Jordan's. By noon, I was on my way to the nearest Fed Ex with my packages and a two hundred dollar money order for my grandmother. Although she never asked me for money, I was sure that she could use it since she was on a fixed income. It also lessened the guilt.

My grandmother was approaching eighty so my family gave me a lot of grief for leaving my kids with her.

"She's too old, she's raised enough kids, and you should be ashamed of yourself to burden her with your responsibilities", were a few of the comments I heard on a regular basis. They were right. She had raised or cared for just about every one of her grandkids and great-grandkids at some point or another. My youngest son made the fourth generation. I had just recently learned that we were now five generations strong thanks to one of my younger cousins. They ran the guilt speech on me every few months, but what if my kids weren't there? She would most likely be alone. To me, it was a win-win situation, but no one else saw it that way.

With my packages sent, I decided to enjoy the rest of my day off relaxing in my new home. However, it didn't take long for me to realize I had too much time on my hands to think about my jacked up past as well as my present state. I've never been proud of my profession because regardless of the money, in my heart I knew it was wrong. But how else could I make the type of money I was making? I rolled my last joint quickly so that I could get the negative thoughts out of my mind. Being high didn't get the job done entirely, but it helped. With weed I could get out of bed every morning and sleep at night. I could tell that Lenny didn't approve of my dependence on the substance, but after I told him the partial truth about why I smoked, he understood. I gave him small bits and pieces about my past, which painted the picture of a typical dysfunctional family.

70

Basically, I included enough information to make him chill on the lectures about the dangers of drugs after all, it was just weed. Now his only request is that he supplies it for me and that I stay away from the hard stuff.

"Sierra, be careful, everyone knows that marijuana is a gateway drug."

This man can't be real. I must have died and gone to heaven.

Things were going as planned and Lenny stuck to our 60/40 deal, which meant that I was doing extremely well financially. After six months of working for him, I had the number two spot in the organization while Janell held down the bottom position. Believe it or not, the positions were based on nothing but seniority. There were plenty of girls around when I started but Janell and I were the remaining two from my earlier days with the group. The girls came and went for various reasons. Greed was the most common cause for getting the boot from Lenny. Some of the girls failed to recognize a good situation and made the mistake of trying to maintain a hustle on the side. Little did they know, even the suspicion of carrying on a side gig was enough for dismissal. One girl actually ended up in the morgue as a result of a side gig. Another girl, (a blue-eyed blond chick named Cindy) was beaten so badly during a side gig, we barely recognized her. The broken heart tattoo on her left breast was actually the only recognizable thing on her body as she lay in the hospital bed with her face bandaged and her eyes swollen to the point that they were almost closed. Lenny paid for the plastic surgery that was needed to restore some of her beauty and the ability to breathe correctly through her nose. The gesture led us to believe that Lenny might be inclined to bend the rules for Cindy. As it turns out, we were wrong. She received her walking papers as soon as she was released from the hospital. We were all disappointed because we really liked her. I was elected by the other girls to talk to Lenny regarding his decision to let her go. That was the first time Lenny ever raised his voice to me.

"Sierra, she knew the rules! Some of these white hoes think they can do whatever the hell they want, but not in this camp. She's out and I don't want to hear another word about it from you or anyone else, you heard me?"

Whenever Lenny was angry or passionate about something, his south Louisiana accent thickened and sometimes I couldn't understand what he was saying. In this particular case, I got half of what he was saying, I got the message loud and clear. I immediately dropped the subject. Damn Cindy, I thought to myself. She would probably end up on the street alone or get picked up by some low classed pimp who would have her working for pennies.

As I became better acquainted with Lenny, I understood his reasons for dismissing Cindy and his attitude toward the White people in general. As a product of the south, "in the era of so-called post-segregation", as Lenny would often say, "the rules changed a little, but the struggle is the same." All of his actions and reactions were based on this concept. As a matter of fact, Lenny had the whole world figured out according to the game of chess with an interesting Black/White perspective. I realized what a brilliant mind Lenny had when he asked me to read one of his college essays:

In the game of chess, there are serious racial overtones. Metaphorically, the different chess pieces can be used to represent different classes or races of people. The movement capabilities (power) of each piece are based on a predetermined set of rules and characteristics. However, there are obstacles/factors that cannot be altered. These obstacles/factors may be detrimental to the achievement of one's goals, as a result, success is determined by an individual's ability to overcome the obstacles/factors.

Interestingly, in the game of chess there is a White team and a Black team. According to the rules of the game, White moves first and therefore has a perpetual and innate advantage over Black. Consequently, Black is automatically placed in a position of defense and forced to do three things in order to survive: develop dynamic counter play, neutralize White's advantage, and achieve equality.

As in chess, there is also an overall objective/goal in the game of life. To play the game successfully from a tactical standpoint, one should concentrate on short-term actions that facilitate long-term goals. In essence, through one's actions/moves or decisions in life, an individual can control his or her own destiny. Further relating to the game of chess an individual's station in life is directly related to the choices made regarding the circumstances that life presents....

In the game of chess a pawn is the lowest representation of power. The rook, the bishop and the knight are more powerful than the pawn, but they are limited by the fact that they can only move in certain directions and under certain conditions. As a result, the individual power of the rook, the bishop and the knight is determined by moment to moment circumstances. The most powerful piece in the game of chess is the queen, followed by the king. Being the most powerful piece, the queen has the ability (freedom) to move in all directions without restriction. The queen is therefore in a position to determine or control her own destiny, however, her main objective is to protect her king.

In the author's opinion, everyone has the ability to become kings or queens. An individual's response to life's obstacles and circumstances will determine one's station in life: King or queen versus pawn, rook, bishop, knight.....

After reading it a few times and identifying the vast number of similarities between pimping and chess, I came to an astonishing conclusion: in spite of the seemingly powerful position, pimps were as powerless as the king and we, "the working girls", were really in a position to control our own destinies. So how then, did we become pawns? I suppose the answer to that question was pretty simple. Successful pimping begins with the mind. A pimp's ability to take a woman's individual weaknesses or circumstances and turn them into real or perceived problems that only he could solve was paramount to his success. I took this information and stored it for daily reference.

In addition to the greed factor, a few of the other girls were dismissed for getting strung out on dope or for disobeying the condom rule. So far, I'd managed to stay in the drama free zone and now that I was his number two girl, I got to spend more time with Lenny. In spite of the fact that I had more miles on my body than anyone could imagine, Lenny never treated me as such. He was without a doubt, the kindest man I had ever known. Inwardly, I acknowledged my feelings for him early in our relationship, but I think I fell in love with him when he told me the story about Tiffany and how much I reminded him of her. Everything made sense after that. The angle that I initially thought he was working wasn't an angle at all. I simply reminded him of the only girl he ever loved.

Sometimes I wondered if Al ever found anyone to remind him of me since he claimed I was the only woman he ever loved. I believed him. In fact, I believed him to the point that I left my own children, moved with him to Dallas and worked two jobs in order to help him take care of his five kids. I never complained. For me, he was *the one* and I would have done anything for him. Sadly, from time to time, I did. If we came up short on the rent or some other bill, he'd ask me to "hang out" with some of his friends. Why would anyone in their right mind agree to something like that? It's simple, I loved him more than I loved myself. It all came to an end when I came home early from work one day and found him in bed with one of his best buddies. I couldn't believe it, and to make matters worse, he was on the bottom. After allowing Al to disrespect me for so many years, I discovered my man wasn't really a man. Perhaps he told the truth when he said I was the only woman he ever loved, however, he never mentioned his attraction to men. Of course, I knew all about down-low brothers and could think of a few back home. I was always critical of the women who found themselves in these relationships and blamed them for their inability to see what everyone else was able to see. Having the proverbial shoe on the other foot was a very humbling experience for me. I can honestly say, I never saw it coming. After that experience, I was more than qualified to give a few lessons on the detection of brothers on the down low.

I left that day with nothing but the clothes on my back, my six hundred and fifty dollar paycheck from the senior citizen home, and the three hundred dollars that I kept hidden in case of an emergency. After wandering aimlessly in the city for a couple of hours, I recalled an ad that I came across at work. A Las Vegas based company was in search of females who were interested in providing companionship for the elderly. The job paid twenty dollars an hour and provided room and board, but I was still somewhat hesitant. My heart was telling me to go home and face my family. However, pride was the mitigating force that stood between me and my family. I couldn't move back home until I had something tangible and worthwhile to take with me. While my family was quite aware of the fact that I was smarter than Alex, no one ever expected me to do anything worthwhile with my life or come anywhere close to being as successful as Alex. How did she manage to overcome all of the things we went

75

through as kids? I just didn't get it. At thirty-two, she was single with no kids, owned a house in DC, a condo somewhere in South Texas, and a fleet of luxury cars. Her only flaw seemed to be her inability to keep a man. But with so many other assets, who needed one? In spite of her professional success, it bewildered me to find that her humility was still intact. Over the years, it became obvious to me that her efforts were sincere. As much as I missed my children, I couldn't go home until I had some tangible evidence of a successful life. It was the burning desire for success that influenced my decision to change professions once I got to Vegas. Just one more year, I thought, as I rolled another joint, and I could go home with my head held high...

Chapter Six

Latrice

Jimmy finally gave up on me. He caught me hiding out in the twenty-four hour crack house providing oral services to a fat white man.

"Jimmy, I did it because you wouldn't give me any money," I said totally convinced that my husband was to blame for my current situation. I knew I was reaching, but hell, I was desperate.

"So this is what you do when I don't give you money? What else have you been doing for money, Latrice? People have been telling me things about you for years but I didn't believe it. I guess I had to see it for myself," Jimmy growled through clenched teeth.

"I'm going to your mother's to see J.T. and when I get home I want your trifling ass out of my house."

"Whatever Jimmy, you don't mean that. Besides, where the hell am I supposed to go?"

He grabbed me around my neck and squeezed as if my neck was one of those rubber stress balls. His voice was still low and controlled, but the veins in his neck had doubled in size and he trembled with anger. However, it was the look in his eyes that scared me the most. Sheer hatred.

"Latrice, you ruined my life, but I loved you anyway. You made me the laughing stock of this whole damn town, but I stayed with you because I wanted our son to have a mother and a father."

I could feel the grip he had on my neck start to loosen but the look on his face and the hatred in his eyes remained.

"If you're not out of my house when I get back you will leave in a body bag."

His words were spoken with conviction, and I knew without a doubt, he was serious. So this was how it was going to play out? That's what I was thinking when he pushed me away. I landed in a puddle of mud face first, providing a perfect visual display of my current state of mind. At that moment, I felt lower than dirt. Jimmy was half way down the street by the time I finally managed to get up. As I stood there assessing the damage to my face with my hands, I noticed the ten dollar bill the guy had thrown at me as he ran for his life. All of this for a measly ten dollars

I went to my house and packed as many things as I could carry and practically ran to my sister's house. I figured she would put me up for a few days or at least long enough for me to come up with a plan. I was officially homeless, I thought, as I approached my destination. I hadn't dealt with this type of problem since I met Jimmy close to ten years ago.

As I stood outside my sister's house, I smoked my last rock under the veil of night and smiled when I thought about the hundred and twenty dollars I had in my pocket thanks to Jimmy. He must have forgotten to take it when he left the house to come looking for me. I knew he saved for a bus ticket to some rehab place in Missouri, but under the circumstances, I didn't have a choice. Surely, he would understand. I planned to go back to the house the next day after Jimmy went to work to see if I could find something worth taking to the pawn shop. The TV and VCR were long gone, but we had a microwave and a few cd's that might be worth a few dollars.

After enjoying my last hit, I knocked on my sister's door a few times before she finally answered. Kathy had an attitude of course, but after hearing that Jimmy had just threatened my life and seeing the scars and bruises on my face, she reluctantly agreed to let me stay for a few days. The next day, I arrived at my former home in time to see Jimmy leave. Thankfully, he didn't see me. As soon as he was out of doubling back distance, I crept around back and used my key to get in the house. Just as I thought, the microwave was the only thing worth taking. Ten years of marriage and the microwave was all we had to show for it.

Jimmy was going to rehab again and with me out of the picture, I had a feeling he would make it this time. J.T. would remain with my parents. There was no sense in me staying around to remind everyone of our disgraceful life. Therefore, I decided to leave, out of sight, out of mind. I met this truck driver named Randy at my usual place of business (behind the washateria/crack house) a few months ago and he swore that he was in love with me. After providing him with the best services that twenty dollars could buy, he begged me to leave my husband and move with him to Arkansas. I said no of course, but I took his number and promised to see him as often as I could. He became one of my most reliable customers. I called him after collecting my forty dollars from the pawnshop. I told him that I'd left my husband and was ready to join him on the road. Three hours later, I was on my way to Arkansas. Before I left, I gave my sister a slip of paper with Randy's phone number on it, just in case something happened while I was gone. After listening to my sister's rant for about as long as I could stand, I headed over to my mother's house to see my son. I kissed him and held him close for a few moments and told him to be good.

"But mommy, why can't you just stay here with us, Grandma said it was okay?" J.T. wailed. In spite of the emotional outburst, I stood there and literally chose crack over my son.

"Sweetheart, mommy has to go. Remember what I told you about the new job I got? It's in another state, but as soon as

I save some money and find a new house, I'm coming to get you," I lied.

He was a kid and there was plenty of time for him to learn the truth about me. For now, I just wanted him to have positive thoughts even if they were based on lies.

When Randy picked me up from the washateria, he immediately made me aware of his expectations, which were primitive to say the least. I was his woman and he expected me to satisfy his every need. In return, he would provide me with food, clothes and shelter. Most importantly, he understood my other needs. While he hated drugs, he was not opposed to providing them for me. Randy was around forty-five or fifty years old and weighed close to three hundred pounds. He had this dirty gray beard and wore a long greasy ponytail. The combined effect was a sinister, redneck, hillbilly appearance. To make matters worse, his personal hygiene was seriously challenged and he listened to country music. However, the potential deal breaker for me was the fact that his socioeconomic views were about as racist as you could get. I never understood how a redneck hillbilly with such fanatically conservative views could be attracted to an African-American crack head. In the end, I weighed my options and there weren't many. So in spite of his negative qualities, I decided to give it a try, at least until something better came along. We developed an understanding and set limits. We wouldn't discuss race or religion, and I would hold up my end of the deal.

For close to two years, we traveled coast to coast with periodic extended stays in Arkansas. Randy had a cute little house in a small town located a few miles west of the Tennessee state line. It was cool being there for a few days, but I enjoyed being on the road because it eliminated the need for domestic activities like cooking and cleaning. On the road, I met Randy's expectations and stayed high enough to forget about home.

I called my mom every Saturday to check on J.T. and to let them know I was still among the living. Jimmy was out of rehab and according to my mom he was working and dating some church lady. He was also in the process of divorcing me and trying to get sole custody of J.T. At that point, it didn't really matter to me as long as J.T. was happy, but my mom was totally against it. She planned to fight Jimmy tooth and nail.

By then, J.T. was almost ten. He was doing well in school and from all indications appeared to be unaffected by the misfortune of being born to unfit parents. I was never really keen on religion, however, I was brought up to believe that Jesus listened to everyone, including sinners like me. My daily prayer was for Him to watch over and protect my son. For a while, it seemed that God listened to me. However, I was sadly mistaken.

My son's life changed completely one afternoon while visiting a friend down the street from my mom. Apparently, this was his daily routine and the family must have been okay or my mom never would have let him spend time at their home. J.T.'s friend had an older brother, who was around fifteen or sixteen at the time. The rotten bastard tried to rape my son. When J.T. got home that evening, he was crying hysterically. My mom asked him over and over again to tell her what happened. When she finally got him to stop crying, he just sat in silence and stared at the floor. She put J.T. in the car, still unaware of the actual circumstances, and drove to the boy's house. No one was home except J.T.'s friend, who cried and pointed to his older brother's room. When my mom entered the room, she nearly passed out when she saw the enormous amount of blood all over the bed and on the floor. Instantly, she knew what had taken place in that room. She grabbed the little boy.

"Who did this?!" she screamed.

The little boy looked at her with fear in his eyes and responded, "My brother."

"Where is he?" my mom demanded.

"I don't know", the little boy innocently replied and my mom believed him.

"Where is your mother?"

"She's at work and so is my daddy."

"Come on, I'm taking you with me to the doctor".

She grabbed both boys and hurried to the car. After waiting two hours in the emergency room, the doctor dispelled my mother's fears. Thankfully, the teenaged pervert had failed in his attempt to violate my son. The blood in the room was due to the broken nose that J.T. sustained during his struggle to defend himself. My mom was relieved, but the doctor still had to give her a sedative to calm her down.

Eventually, they managed to contact my sister Kathy and when she arrived, she wasn't any better. By then, the boy's mother was there and she had the nerve to defend her oldest son, asking if there was any evidence to prove the allegations. It took the doctor and three nurses to keep Kathy away from the woman. When asked if she knew where he was, she said no and refused to allow the physician to examine her youngest son. Instead, she took him and left the hospital. When she got home, police officers were taking pictures of the crime scene and her son sat in the back of a squad car. My mother remained at the hospital with J.T., who had to undergo treatment for his injuries. My dad kept me abreast of things as they unfolded. From what I could hear over the phone, the police showed up just in time or my dad would have been the one in hand cuffs.

According to J.T., the young pervert had made some inappropriate comments to him in the past. As a result, J.T. was careful not to visit his friend when the brother was around. If the brother showed up while he was there, he would just leave, but he was unable to get away this time. I was just thankful that J.T. was able to defend himself. While the outcome could have been far worse, he would still have some psychological issues to deal with as a result of the experience. I wasn't an expert on abuse, but the shame and guilt associated with it was something I understood all too well. I figured there were other psychological issues specific to male victims that would have to be addressed. The social worker gave my mother some contact numbers for an abuse crisis center and urged her to get J.T. into therapy immediately. Hopefully, she would follow through. Most likely, everyone would proceed as if nothing ever happened and J.T. would suffer in silence, as I had.

When I heard about the ordeal, I fell into the worst depression of my life. I was angry, hurt, homicidal, and suicidal. The guilt was almost unbearable. How could I allow something like this happen to my son after what I'd been through? Or better yet, why would God allow it to happen again?

Randy drove me home after getting my hair and nails done and buying me a couple of new outfits.

"I want your family to know that I'm not mistreating you and that I really care about you", Randy told me when he picked me up from the beauty salon.

I had to admit the transformation was remarkable. I had long given up on my appearance, so the mini makeover made me feel human again. We hit the road the next morning with Randy making me promise to put forth an effort to stay sober during my visit with J.T. We left on Christmas Eve exactly one week after my son's horrible experience. I'd spoken with him on the phone every day and he tried really hard to convince me that he was ok. However, I knew all too well how he must have felt. I just wanted to hug him and kiss him and let him know that it was not his fault.

Chapter Seven

Alex

I was in a particularly reflective mood as I made the drive home for a surprise holiday visit. Christmas was supposed to be a joyous time of celebration, thanksgiving and most of all, family. But over the years, the holiday season had become somewhat of a burden for me because it forced me to reflect on some things that I would rather forget. Bad relationships were at the top of the list. By now, I had come to terms with the fact that my personal life, which was predominately, defined by confusion and disappointment, was a complete and utter disaster. It was increasingly apparent that matrimony and motherhood were not in the cards for me. This reality was hard for me to accept. I was supposed to be someone's wife and mother.

For whatever reason, my past relationships were weighing heavily on my mind when I crossed the Mason Dixon line headed south. My thoughts traveled back to the day that changed my life forever. The day I met Demetrius.

"Alex, when are you gonna come to your senses and realize you're living in a fantasy world? It's been close to four years and you're still calling Lawrence your boyfriend. He's ten thousand miles away and you only see him two or three times a year if you're lucky".

I was simply trying to enjoy a glass of Grand Marnier and listen to the music, but my friend Sheila just had to go and spoil it for me. I knew she meant well but she just didn't understand the dynamics of my relationship with Lawrence and I was tired of trying to explain. I was relieved when she excused herself to the ladies room. Upon return, she was flanked by two really nice looking fellows. Even before she made the introductions, I knew the matchmaking games were about to begin.

"Alex, this is Demetrius. Demetrius, meet my friend Alex."

Demetrius was a dead ringer for the actor Richard T. Jones from the movie "G" and based on my personal interpretations of the novel, he was the embodiment of the character Midnight from Sister Souljah's book *The Coldest Winter Ever*. He stood about six feet tall but his demeanor seemed to add a few inches. His perfectly shaped clean shaven head and the cocoa colored dark chocolate skin was enough to get my attention. But in spite of his personal attributes, I was still channeling some serious attitude when Demetrius and I exchanged handshakes. Sheila was doing too much. I decided it was time to make my feelings clear once and for all before the night was over.

As the fellows proceeded to order another round of drinks, I realized I wasn't doing a very good job concealing my irritation with Sheila. After a couple of drinks, I decided to just relax and try to enjoy the mundane table talk. After all, a little talking never hurt anyone. Before long, we were all on the dance floor doing the Bunny Hop. I couldn't remember the last time I'd had so much fun and I was ready for the next song. But the DJ just had to go and blow it by playing one of Keith Sweat's old school slow jams, "There's a right and a wrong way to love somebody…" I politely excused myself and attempted to leave the dance floor, but Demetrius grabbed my arm.

"Alex, I insist. I promise, I won't bite".

"I don't …"

"You don't have to explain, I know you have a man. Just give me this one dance and I promise I won't bother you again."

Without waiting for my long list of excuses, he swept me into his arms and began leading me around the dance floor. He was an extremely graceful dancer with a real knack for sensual dance. I completely submerged myself in the artistic moment and became oblivious to any and everything around me, except following this stranger across the dance floor. When I opened my eyes at the end of the song, I realized we were the only couple on the dance floor and all eyes were on us. He was definitely smooth I thought and tried to regain my composure. If his game was anywhere close to his dancing skills, I was in big trouble.

By this time, Lawrence had been stationed in Hawaii for about a year and I had only one semester left in law school. When he came home for Christmas that year, I fully expected a ring and a proposal, but it didn't happen. Even his dad was a little perturbed when I told him that I didn't get a ring.

"Alex, I don't know what's wrong with that boy," he told me. "He's gonna mess around and lose you."

"It's okay, Mr. Gardner," I lied, not wanting to reveal my true feelings on the matter. I was beyond disappointed.

"We have an understanding and I don't need a ring to prove anything."

Yeah, right.

In spite of the huge let down, I still believed in the relationship. In order to deal with the disappointment, I constantly reminded myself of the conversation we had on our first date regarding his aversion to getting married before retirement. I understood his reasons for waiting, but at the same time I hoped to change his mind. With his retirement still several years away, my patience began to waver.

Ironically, I met Demetrius two days after Lawrence's return to Hawaii after the holiday visit. It was, without a doubt, the most vulnerable period of my relationship. Although I was brutally honest with Demetrius about my relationship status, he was not impressed. We went out a few times for dinner or a movie and I managed to keep things in perspective. I was actually starting to think that platonic relationships with the opposite sex was more than a myth. Those thoughts were quickly banished when he finally started questioning the legitimacy of my relationship with Lawrence.

We were having a few drinks at his place before heading out to catch a late movie. I liked hanging at his place because his old-school music collection was on point. Sometimes I felt like I was born in the wrong era because of my love for the old school sound. I had my father to thank for my ardent appreciation of music. Demetrius and I clearly shared the same passion.

Bobby Womack's, *"Woman's Gotta Have It"* played in the background. I absolutely loved funky baselines, and this song had one of the funkiest. However, the opening lyrics were ghetto fabulous prose, primitively beautiful, yet profoundly true:

"Do the things to keep a smile on her face, say the things that make her feel better every day"....

"Man you got to stay on your p's and q's, if you don't, the woman you could easily lose..."

I never really knew if the song was a planned introduction to the conversation that Demetrius wanted to have or if it spontaneously triggered his next statement.

"Alex, do you honestly believe this guy is in Hawaii with all those beautiful women doing absolutely nothing?" he asked.

He planted the initial seeds of doubt which would eventually lead me into a perpetual state of confusion.

"Wow. You had me fooled there for a minute. I thought I'd finally met someone with the capacity to respect my situation even if you can't understand it. I can't tell you how many times I've been asked this question. Just to let you know, I rarely bother to justify it with a response. I guess you can call it my line in the sand. However, since you waited so long to ask I feel inclined to give you an answer. It's simple. We have a plan and it's working for us. I choose to believe that Lawrence and I have something special," I paused for a moment as the next song began to play. Another Bobby Womack classic, "*If You Think You're Lonely Now...*." Really? Did he create a playlist for this conversation? I was way past irritated with Demetrius and I felt the need to express my feelings explicitly.

"Being the player that you are, I don't expect you to accept anything I have to say. I know all about your little issues with fidelity. The fact that you cheated on your ex-wife has nothing to do with my relationship with Lawrence. And furthermore, I think it's a little childish for you to use your shortcomings as a measuring stick for everyone else."

That was a little below the belt I suppose, but a few people filled me in on the details about Demetrius and his ex-wife.

"I'm not in the mood to sit here and allow you to abate my relationship. I think it's time for me to go," I said and grabbed my keys to head for the door.

"So tell me Alex, what gives you that impression?"

"What impression?" I asked with genuine confusion.

"You just called me a player. What gives you that impression?"

"Well, first of all, you're pursuing a woman who's happily spoken for..." That was all I could come up with. I couldn't let him know that I entertained gossip about him.

"I'm listening."

"Well, wasn't it the reason for your divorce?"

Silence. I figured it was best if I didn't say anything else on the subject.

"Interesting. Before you go Alex, let me ask you a question. Am I the player or am I setting myself up to be played by the one who is actually being played?"

In spite of the complexity of his little brainteaser, it didn't take me long to get the gist of what he was saying. In fact, the message was loud and clear. I left that day feeling defeated instead of angry. As much as I hated to admit it, his words resonated. Was I giving Lawrence more credit than he really deserved and in essence holding him to a standard that was unfair to both of us? Or had I simply met the one person in this world who could actually cause me to lose sight of the future I thought I was moving toward with Lawrence? Suddenly I found myself questioning the very core of my relationship with Lawrence. Physically, we were apart more than we were together. So in essence, the relationship was built entirely on trust and words. This was nothing new to me. We were very much aware of the intricacies of a long distance relationship and were both determined to make it work. That was the plan. So why was it becoming an issue for me all of a sudden? The answer to that question was quite obvious.

Like always, music would be my refuge. As I drove away, John Mayer spoke to me through the melancholic rhythm and lyrics of one of my favorite songs.

"Gravity.....is working against me. And gravity....wants to bring me down, gravity.....stay the hell away from me."

Demetrius and I chilled for a few days with absolutely no communication. I suppose we both waited for the other person to break the ice. I picked up the phone several times to call him but just couldn't follow through. On the one hand, I was relieved because the physical temptation was becoming harder and harder to resist. On the other hand, I missed Demetrius. I just wanted to hear his voice. In the end, he was the one to put an end to the silent war. With one phone call, we were back at square one. We began seeing each other on a daily basis and as we grew closer, the perceived flaws in my relationship with Lawrence were amplified. In hindsight, I find myself questioning the validity of my concerns. Was my relationship really flawed or was Demetrius the reason for my growing lack of trust and skepticism?

Before long, Lawrence became the focus of my frustration.

"Lawrence, why is it that every time we talk, I have to be the one placing the call?"

I guess my guilt was getting the best of me. I'd spent the night at Demetrius's and after a night of wining and dining, I was in desperate need of some reassurance from Lawrence. Otherwise, my relationship with Demetrius would not remain platonic.

"Well, baby", he said, choosing his words carefully, "maybe it's because you never give me a chance to call and lately whenever I call, you're not there."

He was right. I hadn't been home a lot lately because I was hanging out with Demetrius. However, I justified my behavior by the fact that even before Demetrius came along I was beginning to feel neglected. And after I didn't get a ring for Christmas, those feelings were magnified.

"What's up with you Alex? You haven't been yourself lately and I need you to tell me why?"

I didn't say anything for a moment. I'm a horrible liar. But then again, I couldn't let him turn the tables on me, after all, this was as much his fault as it was mine. And how did I know that he wasn't screwing up as well? The whole thing with Demetrius could have been avoided if he had given me a ring for Christmas. I honestly tried to do the right thing by telling Demetrius about Lawrence on our very first date. In spite of my adamant declaration of love and commitment, he wasted no time commenting on my empty ring finger.

My default response was, "I don't need a ring to prove anything pertaining to my relationship."

Not only did he laugh in my face, he disregarded everything I had to say about it.

"Maybe it's because I'm tired, Lawrence. I have a man who's never around and who expects me to be content with a few words and a visit every three or four months."

"Who's getting into your head Alex?" Lawrence asked calmly.

I couldn't defend myself because I knew that I was wrong. Or was I? Finally, I was able to speak.

"Lawrence, I need more than words. I know we have a plan and I know we're going to be together one day, but what about now? I'm tired of being alone and I'm tired of trying to explain why my man is a million miles away."

"I knew it. You finally let some slick ass brother get into your head. Do you remember what I told you before I left, Alex? I told you that as long as you were being true, you would never have to wonder about me and vice versa. All I can tell you is we have a plan. I'm doing my part and I need you to do yours. Is there anything you need to tell me before I hang up?"

I wanted to tell him that he was right, that there was someone else and he was promising me the world. Instead, I ended the conversation as I always did, "Do you love me?"

"Yes, I love you, Alex."

"You promise?"

"Yes, Alex, I promise."

"How do you know?"

"Because I've laughed and I've cried. Good night, baby."

"Good night, Lawrence."

For the next few days I gave Demetrius the cold shoulder. Lawrence was right. We had a plan and I was being lead in another direction. I just needed to be patient and remain focused. But Demetrius was the master of seduction and he didn't hold anything back. From massaging my feet when I got home, to cooking me brownies and washing my car, he methodically peeled away every layer of my resistance. After several months, I still refused to make love and he didn't force the issue. It was a player move no doubt. Nevertheless, his solution to the problem simply added to my confusion. The solution, which was a selfless act in every sense, resulted in the release of my sexual frustration while Demetrius was left to manage his own frustrations through a series of cold showers. However, he was not to be deterred and eventually his hard work paid off.

For two years, I was trapped in a web of confusion, uncertainty, and deceit. At times, I truly believed I was in love with two men. While Demetrius knew about Lawrence, Lawrence knew nothing of my relationship with Demetrius. When Lawrence finally completed his assignment in Hawaii, he immediately asked me to marry him. Although I had dreamed of the day when I would hear those words, I felt none of the joy that I thought I would feel. By now, Demetrius and I were completely immersed in our own little world and I was finally forced to make a decision. But for the life of me I couldn't choose. Finally, the confusion and guilt became too overwhelming. The thought of hurting either of them was more painful than the prospect of being alone. It was the only choice that made any sense. I returned the beautiful princess cut solitaire to Lawrence with a letter, which was supposed to explain my actions. A few days later, I ended my relationship with Demetrius.

Demetrius got married a couple of years after our break-up. I was happy for him but I would be lying if I said it didn't bother me. Lawrence finally retired and moved to Florida, which had always been the plan. He managed to land his dream job and it came with a six-figure salary. Apparently, he took my advice to complete his college degree before he left the military. Surprisingly, he was still single and we kicked it from time to time. In fact, he was in DC on a pretty regular basis--no strings of course. Perhaps there was still hope for us.

Seventy-six miles to my Granny's....

Chapter Eight

Sierra

So far, I had close to two hundred and fifty thousand dollars stashed away in several bank accounts. Business was good, I worked less, and I had a few long standing clients who paid me more than enough to make up the difference. On top of that, Lenny didn't give me a chance to spend my own money. He gave me any and everything I ever wanted and he was constantly trying to get me to retire. But I wasn't ready.

From a financial standpoint, I couldn't return home for good, but I could definitely make a statement. Lenny agreed that a visit with my kids was long overdue, so we made plans to go home for Christmas. I was excited about my visit, but I was also apprehensive. I hadn't been home in two years.

Ironically, the last visit coincided with the sudden death of Keith's mother, Beatrice. According to my mom, she died of a massive heart attack. Over the years, Keith managed to thoroughly humiliate her on a consistent basis. I guess it finally got the best of her. As it turns out, my cousins and I were not the only ones to suffer at the hands of that sick bastard. Apparently, two of my younger cousins, Yasmin and Yori, were victimized as well. Yasmin and Yori were identical twins and absolutely gorgeous. Like the incident with me, it was swept under the rug. Being sixteen at the time of discovery and caught in the act, did little to help their cause. In the biggest scandal to ever hit our little town, the trio was caught red handed in an abandoned shed by some neighborhood kids. When questioned, Yasmin and Yori denied any earlier experiences with Keith, but I knew they were lying. Nine months later, Yori gave birth to Keith's daughter who miraculously suffered no obvious birth defects. She dropped out of school and married her high school sweetheart. He accepted the baby as his own, and they were now living in Texas. Yasmin, on the other hand, became very good friends with Latrice. Once again, Keith managed to escape any punishment for his perverted behavior. While Yasmin and Yori were criticized for being strumpets, as my grandmother so eloquently described, Keith was only mildly ridiculed.

Beatrice was once an outspoken and well respected person in the small community. After hearing about the Yasmin and Yori fiasco, she became a recluse. She stopped going to church, didn't interact with her neighbors, and avoided all contact with the family. She obviously blamed herself. In return, the family simply ignored her. Their actions probably intensified Beatrice's guilt. Cowards. That's the only word I can think of to adequately describe my family and their inability to face conflict.

The tension at Beatrice's funeral was so thick that you could have cut it with a knife. Her daughters had once been like sisters to my mother and my aunts, but in the midst of this tragedy, they all acted like strangers and no words were exchanged between them. Keith was inconsolable and cried like a baby throughout the service. At one point, I made eye contact with him and despite my anger, I couldn't help but feel his sorrow. That was the last time I saw him. However, I heard that he married and had a son. His wife, I'm sure, was completely unaware of the fact that her new husband was a pedophile. Cowards again. How could anyone allow her to wed someone like Keith? Someone in the family should have taken it upon themselves to disclose that bit of information via anonymous call or letter or something. It would have been the right thing to do.

Lenny and I arrived at my grandmother's house and surprised everyone as planned. My kids were delighted with of all the cool things I brought them and my grandmother was excited as well. I brought her a fancy new church dress with a hat, earrings, purse and shoes to match. I gave my mom a pair of diamond earrings and just as expected, she immediately looked on the back for a price tag. Of course, I left it in place because I wanted her to know that I spent fifteen hundred dollars for them. For my aunts, I had two hundred dollar gift certificates to Dillard's. It was definitely a new and gratifying experience for me. It felt good to be the one giving for a change.

Lenny just sat back and took everything in. He told me later that my family was nothing like he expected. To him, they appeared to be close and loving and he couldn't understand why I would go to such lengths to distance myself from them. At that moment, I decided it was time to come clean about my past. Just as I turned around to tell him the truth, I looked down the road and saw a black Mercedes coming toward the house. It was Alex. I immediately lost the spotlight when she stepped out of the car dressed in black from head to toe and looking extravagant as ever. And in typical Alex fashion, she was loaded down with gifts for everyone. Apparently, she was on her way to a conference in Dallas and on a whim, decided to surprise everyone. Of all the times I could have chosen to come home for a visit, why did it have to coincide with hers? I don't know why, but she always made me feel so small. Even the mention of her name was enough to put me on edge, but this time would be different. I had money, nice clothes, and a drop dead gorgeous man at my side. She was glamorous as usual, but just like always, she was alone. Lenny noticed the sudden change in my attitude and wanted to know who Alex was and why I didn't like her. I shot daggers at him with my eyes while I gave Alex a fake hug and exaggerated greeting.

"Hey girl, how have you been? Where are you living these days?" I asked.

I tried to give an impression of true interest, when in reality, I couldn't care less.

"Maryland for now, but I'm thinking about moving closer to home. City life is starting to get old. What about you, Sierra?"

"Las Vegas. Oh, forgive me Alex, this is my friend Lenny. Lenny this is my cousin Alex."

Alex looked like she'd just seen a ghost.

"Lenny," she repeated his name slowly and then realized she was staring.

"Sorry," she said apologetically. "You bear a striking resemblance to someone I knew a long time ago."

"As a matter of fact, you two could be brothers. Where did you say you were from?"

As Lenny reached for her hand and gave a firm handshake, he looked her squarely in the eyes.

"I didn't, but I'm from South Louisiana and it's a pleasure to finally meet you. Sierra has told me a lot about you."

That was actually true, but I wished he hadn't said it. I didn't want Alex to think that I lived vicariously through her.

"So what brings y'all down this way?"

Alex asked the question with an exaggerated southern drawl. You would think that with all of her education and travel, she would have gotten rid of the country tone by now.

"No reason, I just decided to surprise everyone," I replied.

"How long are you going to be here?" I asked.

"Just a few days; I took some time off to sort of clear my head. I figured a road trip would give me some time to think. Benz loves to ride," she said and gave her eight-year old dog a pat on the head.

"When are you guys leaving?"

"Oh, I don't know."

I answered before Lenny could speak. I had already decided to cut the visit short.

"Day after tomorrow, most likely," I stated firmly.

"Well, we need to hang out before you go, catch up on some things. Nice meeting you Lenny," she said and directed her attention toward the house.

I'm sure she noticed the missing shutters and un-kept yard. Within five minutes, she would have a mop and bucket in her possession. That was just her. Without even trying, she had a way of making people feel absolutely worthless. To be honest, I didn't think she did it on purpose. In spite of her success and affluence, Alex was still Alex. There were a few haters in the family who felt that her long absences were due to her desire to forget her humble beginnings. In my heart, I knew that they were off target. Alex and I distanced ourselves for the same reasons. Underneath that ironclad exterior, I was certain that Alex was just as broken as I was. I wouldn't be surprised if she still woke up screaming in the middle of the night like I did.

Chapter Nine

Alex

Sierra looked great and was obviously doing well, but why Vegas? No one in their right mind would actually choose Vegas as the place to call home, and what was up with this guy Lenny? The name was eerily familiar, but I couldn't recall when or where I'd heard it. Then, all of a sudden it hit me. It was the name that Tiffany kept repeating when she found out she was HIV positive. There was probably no connection. There had to be a million Lenny's in the world, surely he was not the one Tiffany referred to. For one, Tiffany was from Alabama and went to college in Tennessee and this guy was from South Louisiana. He looked like an educated brother, but under the circumstances, I couldn't be certain. The simplest solution to this problem was to find out if he ever attended college and if so, where? I decided to just ask.

Later that evening, I got an opportunity.

"So, Lenny," I began when I noticed the college ring for the first time.

"Where did you go to school and what field did you say you were in?"

Sierra had gone to the car to get some pictures. I wanted to find out as much as I could before she returned.

"Delaney University in Tennessee and I'm a real estate investor. Vegas property is really hot right now. I'm just riding it until it plays out..."

I immediately tuned out the rest of his statement. Delaney University. My heart pounded really fast, but somehow, I was able to remain calm.

"Real estate is an excellent field. Are you into commercial or private property?"

"Both," he said and peered at me with a raised eyebrow.

I wasn't doing a very good concealing my sudden anxiety.

"Okay, Lenny, I need to ask you a really strange question. I don't want you to think I'm crazy, just answer me and I will explain later. Do you know a girl named Tiffany, from Alabama?"

Lenny nearly dropped the can of beer that he held. After a moment he responded.

"Tiffany? Do you mean Tiffany Robinson?"

"Yes, Tiffany Robinson."

I couldn't believe it. What were the odds that this could really be happening? Six degrees of separation. I made a mental note to review the theory again. Maybe there was some truth to it after all.

"How do you know her?"

Lenny demanded to know.

"I met her in the Army" I said slowly, not really sure how to proceed with the conversation.

After a few moments of complete silence, Lenny finally spoke.

"Yes, I know Tiffany. We were at Delaney together."

He paused and continued in a barely audible tone.

"I can't believe she really went through with the Army thing. Alex, where is she? How is she doing?"

He looked visibly shaken, to say the least.

Carefully choosing my words, I spoke.

"When was the last time you spoke to her Lenny?"

How was I going to tell him that this person, whom he obviously cared for very deeply, was dead?

Tiffany contacted me a month before she died to let me know that she had full blown AIDS. She accepted her fate gracefully, spending the last year of her life speaking to college students and warning whoever would listen about the dangers of unprotected sex. She was an excellent speaker and in spite of her condition, she was still a very beautiful girl. To get her message across, she spent the morning on campus in conversation with the male students. She gave her number to those who asked and set up dates for later that night. When she went on stage to give her speech, she would ask all of the guys who had her phone number to stand, along with the guys who planned to go out with her that night. As they stood, she carefully explained to the audience, "The guys who are standing represent the number of individuals who could potentially become exposed to HIV".

"How, you ask? Well I'm HIV positive and I'm sure that I could have kicked it with at least one of the gentlemen that you see standing. HIV is out there, and it doesn't discriminate. It doesn't matter what sorority or fraternity you're in. It doesn't matter if you're having sex with one person or one hundred. Ladies and gentlemen, protect yourselves. If I could go back and change my life, I would, but I can't. So do me a favor, every time you think about having unprotected sex, think about me. I am here to give you a visual picture of the disease and to let you know that it can happen to anyone. Make no mistake. Deception is the weapon of choice for HIV. While you can't see it, I need you to know that it's here and it's real".

That particular speech was given at her alma mater, Delaney. It was hard for her to go back because many of her instructors and ROTC staff members were still there. When she called and asked if I could go with her, I immediately said yes. It would turn out to be her last speech because a month later she collapsed at her mother's home. Tiffany was not surprised to find out her T cell count was dangerously low. She'd stopped taking her anti-viral meds several months ago. According to her, she was tired of fighting a losing battle. I went to see her while she was in the hospital and was totally unprepared for what I saw. In just one month, the breathtakingly beautiful girl with perfect skin was now covered in sores. She had always been tiny, so by this point she probably weighed less than eighty pounds and that was being generous. However, her eyes were the most revealing. What I saw was pain and fear as she stared blindly into my eyes. On top of her chest sat a bible and a pair of reading glasses. She was ready and everyone in the room knew it. I sat with her in silence until early morning. At exactly five thirty a.m., she reached for my hand, smiled, and quietly slipped away. Her mom, who had been with her day and night for the past month, was at home after I insisted that she get some rest. When I called to tell her Tiffany was gone, she spoke gently into the phone.

"I know. I could feel it. Thank you, Alex for being there. I don't think I could have handled it. In the drawer next to her bed, you will find all of the necessary information and phone numbers for the funeral home. I'm just not ready to see my baby lying there lifelessly. She had so much to live for. How did this happen?"

In the span of about thirty seconds, Tiffany's mother completed every stage of loss: reflection, acceptance, and anger. I knew that she was in no shape to handle the logistics. I contacted the funeral home, made the arrangements with the church, picked the casket and the dress, and provided an outline of the funeral program. All Mrs. Robinson had to do was plug in the names for the soloist and the ministers.

Tiffany's dress was white chiffon with long puffy sleeves. I chose it because I thought it would conceal the severity of her suffering and frailty. Her hair was still absolutely beautiful, so I asked the funeral home beautician to style it so that it hung below her shoulders with a red rose placed to the right temple. She looked like a chocolate Barbie doll in her white casket, which was complete with gold trim. In the church, there were so many flowers that the funeral home director had to spread them all over the church. There were hundreds of red roses, red carnations and white lilies. Of all the funerals I'd attended, Tiffany's was by far, the most beautiful. All twelve of her line sisters were there and when they sang the Delta Sigma Theta ritual song, there was not a dry eye in the building.

As my thoughts traveled back to that day, everything around me seemed to fade in to the background. Lenny had to practically scream my name.

"Alex!"

"Oh Lenny" I said completely embarrassed. "I'm sorry, my mind was somewhere else."

"We were talking about Tiffany and you sort of checked out on me for a moment. Are you okay?"

"Lenny, I have to tell you something, but I don't know how."

"Is it about Tiffany? Is she okay?"

Chapter Ten

Latrice

As I turned the corner headed to Granny's, I noticed a couple of unfamiliar cars and faces in the driveway. Hmmm, a party and no one invited me. Last time I checked, I was still a part of this family, and at least, I had the decency to show my face around here more than once every three or four years. The nerve of these people. Who was the cutie sitting next to Alex? Damn, he was fine. Let me guess, another one of her arm pieces no doubt. Poor fellow, I thought. In a couple of months, he would be yesterday's news. Alex had never been able to keep a man. Others see her as being selective, however, I think that she likes the variety and freedom. If I brought a different guy home every time I visited, that's exactly what the family would think about me. As I made my way over to the cute little couple, Sierra surprised me from behind with a big hug.

"Girl, how are you doing? How are J.T. and Jimmy?"

"Good question," I said sharply. "I haven't seen either of them for at least a week, but in our world, no news is good news, if you know what I mean. What's up with you?"

It was really good seeing Sierra. Wow, she looked great. I'd give her twenty-five easily.

"You look great, Sierra. What's your secret?"

"You see that fine ass man over there talking to Alex? That's my secret. He keeps me looking good."

"You mean that specimen over there belongs to you? I assumed he was here with Alex."

I glanced over that way again. They appeared to be in deep conversation, but Sierra didn't appear to be concerned. She obviously had him in check. Otherwise, who in their right mind would leave a man like that alone with Alex?

"Come on, let me introduce you. Baby, this is my other cousin, Latrice. Remember, I told you the three of us grew up like sisters."

Alex seemed a little surprised at Sierra's description of our relationship. I just gave Lenny a big toothless grin and a lingering handshake.

"So, what brings the two of you all the way down here at the same time? The only time we see you is when someone dies."

They knew I was telling the truth. Sierra answered first.

"Lenny and I made a last minute decision to head this way for the holidays."

"Same here," Alex said with a strange look on her face. "I had a few days off and decided to hit the road. What's up with you, Latrice?"

"Oh, you know how things are around here, same whore, different dress. Nothing new. I'm just trying to keep J.T. in line as best as I can, but he's like every other sixteen year old. He thinks he knows everything. Just last week, he came home with a pocket full of money and no explanation for where he got it."

I left out the fact that he gave me a small portion of it. I wasn't proud of the fact that a mere fifty dollars could buy my motherhood. Why was Sierra looking at me like that? Had someone already given her the scoop on what was really going on or was she checking out my grill? I know I've missed a couple of dental appointments, but after all the drama I've been through, I think I still look pretty damn good. Guess it's time for me to bounce before Alex started asking too many questions and offering solutions for all of my problems. My answer was still the same. No, I don't want to go to rehab. I'm doing just fine. And no, I'm not interested in getting my GED.

"Nice to meet you Lenny. I'll see you all later. I've got some business to attend."

As I walked away, I could feel their eyes on me. This is exactly the kind of thing I'm talking about. Those two were the biggest hypocrites I'd ever seen. On the outside, they appeared to have it all together, but on the inside, they are just as jacked up as I am or worse.

Sierra

"Wow, I can't believe Latrice is still getting high after all these years. How does she do it?"

I mumbled to no one in particular. Alex had that familiar look in her eyes. The look of reflection, I suppose you could call it. It was always followed by a trip into the past.

Quietly, she asked, "What's stopping her?"

I knew where she was going with that question, but I was just not ready to have that conversation. Besides, Lenny only knew a few of the details about my horrible childhood and this was not a good time to fill him in on the rest. So, I changed the subject.

"Alex, why don't you join us for dinner tonight? We're going to this new seafood place on the boardwalk. It's supposed to be the bomb."

"Sure, Sierra, what time?"

Alex responded with very little enthusiasm. What was eating her? Her attitude was totally different after the short conversation she had with Lenny.

"Just meet us here at eight and we'll ride together."

"OK, I'll be here."

Alex excused herself and marched back over to Granny's house. That's when I noticed the change in Lenny's mood. I was accustomed to his frequent mood swings, but there was something different this time. Alex must have said something to him. If she had so much as uttered one word about me to Lenny, I was going to kick her ass.

"Baby what's wrong? Did Alex say something about me?"

"No," Lenny said quietly. "Your cousin knows Tiffany."

"Who?"

"Tiffany."

"You mean Tiffany, the girl from college?"

My voice cracked in my complete shock. As he walked away, I quietly finished my thought, "the only girl you ever loved, the one who broke your heart."

Surprisingly, he heard me and responded.

Well, if that's how you want to put it. I haven't seen her in over ten years. Last I heard, she planned to join the Army after graduation. Something is going on with her. Alex was about to fill me in before you and your cousin came over.

Tiffany... just what I needed. I always suspected that he still loved her, but how much? Talk about bad timing. Just when I thought Lenny and I were going to move on to the next level, along comes Alex with this Tiffany drama. Of all the people in the world, how did Alex manage to make the acquaintance of Lenny's ex-girlfriend? To my knowledge, Alex never attended Delaney. So, how could this happen?

"Well, maybe you can talk to her about it tonight over dinner," I said. I tried really hard to hide my irritation, but I failed miserably. "I'm sure Alex will tell you everything."

"Yeah, you're right. It can wait."

Chapter Eleven

Alex

For all intents and purpose, the "six degrees of separation theory" was proving to be more than just a myth. According to this theory, an individual can be linked with anyone in the world through a series of no more than six personal connections.

I was glad for the interruption in my conversation with Lenny. I still hadn't come up with the right words to tell him about Tiffany's death and her final years. In the weeks following her last speech at Delaney, I spoke with Tiffany by phone every day. Over a period of about one month, we became best friends. My biggest regret was that I was not there for her in the beginning. As fate would have it, I could now fulfill one of her last wishes. In one of our last conversations, she mentioned a letter she'd written to Lenny. Apparently, writing was her personal therapy because there were a number of diaries in the nightstand beside her hospital bed. That's where I found the letter addressed to Lenny. I have to admit, curiosity almost got the best of me, but out of respect for Tiffany's privacy, I resisted the urge to read it. I also went a step further and made no mention of the letter to her mom. Tiffany's mom was a wreck. The last thing that she needed was to find out some other deep dark secret about her child. I simply held on to the letter, never thinking in my wildest dreams that I would have an opportunity to actually deliver it. Like never before, I believed my friend Camilla's theory. According to her, some people are placed in your life for a season while others enter your life for a reason. In light of our brief relationship, it seemed my purpose for meeting Tiffany so many years ago was to fulfill one of her last wishes.

I left my grandmother's house at around two that afternoon and made my way to Camilla's house. Over the years, it had become customary for me to stay with her whenever I was in town. It gave us a chance to catch up on personal events and local gossip. I had some other old friends who were still around, but my relationship with them had changed over the years. We had been friends since kindergarten, went to the same college, shared our hopes and dreams and provided reality checks for each other whenever necessary. By the time I finally reached her house, I was mentally and physically exhausted. After we shot the breeze for a few minutes, I ran down the details of my current dilemma regarding Tiffany and Lenny. After she heard my story, Camilla agreed that I had no choice in the matter. I had to tell him. I was not surprised by her final thoughts on the subject.

"Alex, to all things there is a purpose. Some people enter your life for a season while others enter your life for a reason," we recited in unison.

I smiled. We knew each other so well. I was still nervous about the situation, but after talking it over with Camilla, I was more optimistic about the outcome.

I decided to take a quick nap before meeting Sierra and Lenny. I woke up at around six and took a long hot shower. After I dried the dampness away from my body and applied my favorite lotion, I opened all three suitcases and carefully reviewed my options. I decided on an ultra-conservative ensemble. I figured being *too* fly might offend Sierra in some way. I could tell by the way she clung to Lenny that she was definitely insecure, but who could blame her? He was extremely easy on the eyes.

By the time I finally reached Camilla's, I was mentally exhausted. After we shot the breeze for a few minutes, I ran down the details of my current dilemma regarding Tiffany and Lenny. After she heard my story, Camilla agreed that I had no

109

choice in the matter. I had to tell him. I was not surprised by her final thoughts on the subject.

"Alex, to all things there is a purpose. Some people enter your life for a season while others enter your life for a reason," we recited in unison.

I smiled. We knew each other so well. I remained nervous about the situation, but after talking it over with Camilla, I was more optimistic about the outcome.

I decided to take a quick nap before meeting Sierra and Lenny. I woke up at around six and took a long hot shower. After I dried the dampness away from my body and applied my favorite lotion, I opened all three suitcases and carefully reviewed my options. I decided on an ultra-conservative ensemble. I figured being *too* fly might offend Sierra in some way. I could tell by the way she clung to Lenny that she was definitely insecure, but who could blame her? He was extremely easy on the eyes.

Sierra

My stress level was at an all-time high. I still couldn't believe Alex was somehow acquainted with Tiffany, of all people. Was this another one of God's painful lessons in the trials and tribulations of life or was this just proof that Lenny and I are destined to be business associates and nothing else? While waiting for Alex to arrive, I scrutinized my appearance in search of even the smallest imperfection. After I changed my outfit four or five times, I was finally pleased and thoroughly convinced that I was as fly as possible. I also in need of a last minute ego boost, so I decided to get Lenny's opinion, However, he was completely oblivious to me. He sat quietly in front of the TV with his eyes closed and his head thrown back on the recliner.

"Lenny what do you think?" I asked.

I desperately wanted to regain some of his attention. I chose a little black dress which was sleeveless and showed off my well defined arms. The hemline hovered around the middle of my thighs. I had to admit, the dress left little to the imagination, but it provided enough coverage to ensure my respectability.

Without looking, Lenny gave me his approval.

"You look great Sierra."

At that point, I knew my relationship with Lenny was in serious trouble.

"Do you still love her?"

He lifted his head and stared at me for a moment.

His soft reply, "I don't know," sent chills down my spine.

Alex

Satisfied that my makeup was applied to absolute perfection, I looked at the clock and realized it was past seven. It would be impossible for me to make it back to Granny's in time to meet Sierra and Lenny, so I called Sierra for the address and told her to meet me at the restaurant. After thinking about it, I decided it was probably a good idea to have my own transportation.

I was first to arrive. Instead of going in alone, I waited in the car and tried to collect my thoughts. I spotted Sierra and Lenny a few minutes later, and we all walked in together. We found a secluded area in the back and immediately started ordering drinks, vodka and cranberry juice for me, crown on the rocks for Sierra and water for Lenny. Without further ado, Sierra demanded to know what was going on with Tiffany and why it was so important at this point in everyone's life.

"Sierra, chill," Lenny said without trying to hide his irritation.

Alex took a deep breath and began.

"Ok, guys, here's the deal. I met Tiffany almost nine years ago in Colorado. We were both there on our first military assignment."

"Yes, I heard she joined the Army. To be honest with you, I didn't think she'd actually go through with it. I'm proud of her. Where is she now?"

Lenny asked with genuine concern for this woman who once meant the world to him. Sierra kept quiet but managed to get her point across through body language. She was totally not feeling this conversation.

"Lenny, I am at a loss for words and I have racked my brain trying to figure out exactly how to tell you...."

"Alex," Sierra hissed as she finished her second drink, "just say it."

Lenny looked at Sierra without a hint of expression, as she continued.

"I'm tired of the drama and I think we need to get whatever it is out into the open so that we can all move on."

"Sierra, I asked you to chill...."

"No, she's right. There's no easy way to say this, so I'm just gonna say it. Lenny, Tiffany is dead."

"Alex, what are you saying? Are you sure we're talking about the same Tiffany? I mean come on, this has to be a mistake…"

I opened my wallet and handed Lenny a picture of Tiffany.

"I'm sorry Lenny, it's her."

Lenny slowly reached for the picture and was visibly shaken when he realized that it was in fact, Tiffany. Sierra sat motionless after taking a look at the picture. I knew that it was like looking into a mirror for her.

"Alex, what happened to her?"

Lenny could barely speak. His voice was thick with emotion.

"AIDS."

"AIDS? You're telling me that Tiffany died from AIDS? How? Was it a needle stick or some freak accident in the hospital?"

Lenny came unglued. I decided against telling him the details, opting instead to tell him about the letter.

"The letter was addressed to you, and I never opened it. It's at home in my closet where I thought it would remain forever."

"Lenny, do you think, I mean is there any way that you….?"

Sierra finally got the nerve to ask Lenny if he was concerned about being infected but he cut her off in mid-sentence.

"No Sierra, I'm clean. You should know that."

The rest of the evening went by in virtual silence with each of us lost in our individual thoughts. As we departed, Lenny and I discussed possible options regarding his receipt of Tiffany's letter. In the end, delivery by mail was out of the question due to Lenny's fear that it would get lost. We exchanged numbers and agreed to meet at some point in the near future in Tuskegee, Alabama, which was Tiffany's home. He wanted to visit her final resting place.

Surprisingly, Sierra was quiet and had very little input during the decision-making process. Obviously distraught by the shocking revelations of the evening, my guess was she needed to collect her thoughts for the conversation that she and Lenny would have once they were alone. By now, Sierra must have understood the delicacy of the situation and realized that her immediate reaction would seriously impact her relationship with Lenny. Could she handle it? Would she be able to console him as he grieved for another woman?

Chapter Twelve

Latrice

Something was obviously going on with the three musketeers. The private, intense conversations made me a little uncomfortable at first because I was usually the topic in such discussions. However, I began to think that something sinister might be going on between the three. I quickly dismissed that idea because Alex just wasn't the type. The unusual behavior continued for the remainder of their visit and by the time they left, my paranoia was through the roof. I was just ready for things to get back to normal.

The thing that I dreaded most about Alex's visits was her inability to resist the urge to bring up the past. True to form, on the night before she left, Alex did just that. Now more than ever she felt the need "do something".

"Alex, we're talking about something that happened twenty years ago. What exactly are you suggesting that we do? And how is it gonna change anything?" I asked, refusing to go along with Alex.

Was Alex crazy enough to think that exposing Keith would somehow erase all of the horrible things that happened? Why couldn't she just let it go?

"You're right Latrice, it won't change anything but maybe it will give us some closure and maybe even a little peace. I've spent the last twenty years trying to deal with this on my own and seeing a shrink once a week for the last five. Nothing works. I don't know about the two of you, but I'm not just angry, I'm mad as hell! And I'm tired of people telling me time heals all wounds. That is absolute bullshit because I'm still hurting!" Alex screamed, not caring anymore if anyone heard her.

Sierra and I looked at each other in disbelief at this rare display of emotion from Alex. She sobbed uncontrollably but was still determined to get her point across.

"Look, I've been thinking about this a lot lately and I've decided I have to do something even if you and Sierra choose not to get involved".

"Ok Alex, what do you suggest we do?" Sierra asked.

"We need to confront him," Alex managed to say in between sobs.

"Ok. I'm down. Let's do it. He's down the street right now and I have a plan."

If we were gonna do it, it had to be right, I thought.

"What's the plan, Latrice?" Sierra asked with more interest. Suddenly, she didn't think it was such a bad idea after all. "I'm in."

"Cool. Meet me at my mom's at eight o'clock tonight. She and my dad went to see BB King, and J.T. is at his girl's house. They won't be home for a while".

"Thanks guys," Alex said while her tears slowly stopped.

"I'll be there," Sierra promised.

If she hurried, she could take Lenny back to the hotel and make it back just in time.

I wasn't exactly sure how I was gonna make it happen, but I was determined. At exactly eight o'clock that night, Keith banged on the door. According to the plan, Alex was to remain in the back room until the appointed time.

As Keith walked into the room, he was noticeably surprised to see Sierra.

"Well, hello, Sierra. Wasn't expecting to see you here."

"I'm sure you weren't."

"Latrice, what's this all about? I thought you called me over here to check out some computers you were trying to unload."

"Yeah, well, I lied. I called you over here to talk about your problem."

"What problem are you referring to, Latrice? You must have me mixed up with someone else. I really don't have time for this. I'll catch you later."

"So Keith, does your wife know that you're a pedophile?"

Sierra asked the question before he could turn to leave.

"Again, you must have me mixed up with someone else. You guys need to get off that stuff. It's obviously messed with your brain. Who would ever believe either of you anyway? It's my word against yours, a crack-head and a Vegas whore," Keith said with a sarcastic grin.

Without waiting for the cue, Alex stepped into the room.

"You think they'd believe me, Keith?"

Just like that, the laughter was gone.

"Alex. Long time no see. What are you doing hanging out with these low-lives?"

"Low lives? Really? And what does that make you, Keith?"

"Look, Alex, you don't have a dog in this fight. Hell, I consider you the one that got away."

Keith smiled with a wicked grin.

"You sick bastard. You think its ok to fondle and rape little girls?"

"They wanted it, Alex. They had to. Didn't you manage to get away?"

"So, you're admitting what you did?" Sierra asked.

"No one else will hear it, so why not?"

Keith responded with an arrogant shrug of his shoulders.

Then, all of a sudden, his demeanor totally changed. His head dropped and he stared at the floor.

"Alex, you're an educated lady. Maybe you can relate to what I'm about to say. Since we're telling shit, we might as well tell it all. It was my grandfather...."

Keith stopped for a moment and took a deep breath.

"Peabody was a sick bastard. He made me what I am today. Make sense now?"

Wow. This family had more drama in it than all of Tyler Perry's movies combined. It made a lot of sense. Most pedophiles were once the victims of the same abuse, but his grandfather of all people? No one said a word. I guess we were all in shock. For a moment, I almost felt sorry for Keith—my abuser. The Stockholm theory; I read about it in one of those books Alex was forever shoving down my throat. If I remember correctly, the theory refers to the tendency of the victim to actually sympathize with the abuser. It only lasted for a moment.

"But Keith, what happened? Did he...?"

"Save the questions Latrice. My wife and son are at home waiting for me. I have nothing more to say. If you decide to repeat a word of what I just said, I'll deny it. Your word against mine."

Just like that any sympathy I had for him was gone.

"It was great seeing you again," he directed to Sierra and Alex.

"Latrice, let me know when you get your hands on the goods. And don't be contacting me with no shit like this."

Without another word, he was gone.

After a few moments of silence, we went our separate ways. I went to my usual place of business to score a much needed fix. This place had become my sanctuary since my split with Randy. I sat in the back room of the old run down house with a pipe in one hand and a lighter in the other. Alex was right. I felt a little lighter after confronting Keith. We should have done this a long time ago.

Chapter Thirteen

Alex

The events from the previous night were surreal. Just hearing Keith's jacked up confession somehow made me feel a little better. If only we could take some type of legal action. Sadly, the statute of limitation for this sort of thing had come and gone years ago. There was really nothing else we could do short of calling a family press conference. Somehow, I didn't think that was a good idea. After all these years, my family was still enamored with Keith. Just yesterday, he had the audacity to show up at my Granny's for the family's farewell get together for me and Sierra.

I didn't think any of us were psychologically prepared to deal with an episode like the one Sierra experienced.

I left Granny's house the next day and continued on to my original destination. Even though I was mentally and emotionally drained, I couldn't come up with any valid reason to ditch the conference. I had been selected to give a series of lectures to a young group of emergency physicians regarding the legal aspects of their profession. I won a huge wrongful death suit down in south Texas last year which received an enormous amount of media coverage. I guess it's the medical-legal version of sleeping with the enemy since I now provided tips on how to avoid a lawsuit. Initially, I was excited to give the lecture and the reimbursement fee was more than adequate, but at this point all I could think about was Lenny and Tiffany.

As I listened to her description of the relationship and saw Lenny's reaction to her death, there was no doubt in my mind that what they had was real. For the life of me, I couldn't figure out how something so special could end so tragically.

119

I reached the Waldorf hotel around noon after checking Benz into the ritzy pet hotel up the street. When I woke up from my nap, I decided to go over my lecture notes for the next day. I discovered my computer charger was not in my bag and spent the next hour searching every piece of luggage over and over while mentally retracing my steps. After giving into the fact that it wasn't in my possession, I contacted Camilla who confirmed my suspicion. It was right where I left it in her office. I called the front desk and spoke to three attendants before I finally got the directions to the nearest Apple store. Surprisingly, there was only one store in the entire city, and it was nowhere close to the hotel. The only other store was fifty miles away in Arlington, Texas. Frustrated, I headed down to the bar and ordered myself a Grand Marnier to clear my head. I needed to figure out a Plan B for my presentation. I had my zip drive and some hard copies of the material. However, I wanted to use the slide presentation because it was so beautifully done.

While at the bar, I struck up a conversation with the gentleman next to me. Before I knew it, we were laughing and having a really good time. For a moment, I completely forgot about everything.

"You know, you should smile more. I wish you could have seen the look you had on your face when you came in here. You looked like you had weight of the world on your shoulders. Whatever it is you're stressing about can't be that bad."

Instead of telling him about the origin of my frown, which had been constant since I was five years old, I gave a simple explanation.

"I left my computer charger at my friend's house in Louisiana and Dallas doesn't seem to be a very Apple-friendly city. I had to talk to three attendants before I could get some information about the nearest store."

He smiled and said that he was actually thinking about buying a MacBook and would love to assist me in my quest to find the nearest store.

"That's very kind of you. I think I'll take you up on your offer. I have my car so all we really need is directions," I said.

I finished my second glass of liqueur and grabbed my purse.

"Umm, I don't think that's such a good idea. We're in a strange city and we've both had a couple of drinks. Why don't we just get a cab," he suggested.

"You know, I think you're right."

As we headed over to the concierge to request a cab, I noticed that he was quite handsome. Within minutes, we were on our way down I-635 to Best Buy. Apparently, the cab driver was also oblivious to the fact that an Apple store even existed. Unbelievable, I thought. On the way, the laughter and pleasant conversation continued. When we approached our destination, the driver asked how long we'd been married. I decided to wait and see how my new friend would respond. When he didn't reply, I laughed.

"Sir, I don't even know this man's name."

"You're kidding me right?"

The cab driver responded in clear disbelief.

"No sir, I'm not," I answered.

I smiled and looked into the eyes of the stranger who sat so close to me that our thighs touched.

"By the way, what is your name?"

"Christopher Carlson, but please call me Chris," he said and grabbed my hand to exit the cab.

After he paid the driver, he turned to me and asked very softly, "What is your name?"

"Alexandra Phillips, but I prefer Alex."

My reply was quick because I was suddenly taken aback by the vibe that developed between us.

"Come on Alex, let's go. I asked the cab driver to wait for us, so we don't have much time."

Sensible thoughts were long gone for me. As absurd as it may seem, I was falling for this guy and I'd only known him for two hours. I must be tripping. It was absolutely ridiculous to have such thoughts going on in my head, but I swear it seemed like I'd known him forever. I was so intrigued by this gentleman that I didn't even trip when we discovered the store had none of the items we wanted. During the cab ride back to the hotel, I started to feel a little nervous tension as my attraction continued to grow. I also wondered how the evening would end.

To my surprise, it ended in the same location that it started, at the bar. We both had another drink and said our awkward goodbyes. I went to bed that night with thoughts of this stranger heavily on my mind. He said he would be in town for a few days. I wondered if I would see him again the next day.

I went downstairs for breakfast a little early the next morning so that I would have time to check out the media equipment in the conference room. I also had to make sure I had enough copies of my presentation, just in case. After I ordered my bagel and a cup of coffee, I performed a quick scan of the room and looked straight into the eyes of my new friend. My eyes lit up so fast, there was nothing I could do to hide the excitement. I hoped the display of emotion was lost in the distance between us. He smiled and made his way to my table from the other side of the room.

"Good morning, Alex. How was your night? Did you sleep well?"

Did I sleep well? Thoughts of my restless night immediately crossed my mind.

"As a matter of fact, I did," I lied. "How about yourself?"

"Well sort of. It takes a while for me to get comfortable when I'm out of my natural element if you know what I mean. There's nothing like sleeping in your own bed."

"Well, perhaps you'll rest a little better tonight."

I realized after a glance at my watch that I had to end the conversation quickly if I was going to check out the equipment before the conference began. Reluctantly, I excused myself and wished him a wonderful day while I scrambled to gather up my things. His eyes were glued to me and my every move. For some reason, I chose that moment to become clumsy. I'm sure I lost all of my cool points when my papers went flying all over the floor. In one swift motion, he picked up my papers and handed them to me.

"See you later Alex," he said and walked away.

I hurried on to the conference room and had just enough time to check out the equipment before the seats began to fill. Thankfully, the media equipment had USB capability, and I was able to present my beautiful slide show. A few minutes into my presentation, I scanned the crowd to see if my audience was captivated or completely bored by the information. Once again, my eyes became locked with Chris'. What was he doing here? Was he stalking me or what? When I was finally done with the question and answer portion of my presentation, I hurried over to find out just what was going on. Before I could say a word, he explained.

"Sorry, Alex. I guess I failed to mention my purpose for being here. I'm an emergency room physician in Chicago and I'm here for the conference. You left out a few things about yourself as well. You're pretty sharp, Ms. Attorney. I'm thoroughly impressed. Where did you go to school? How long have you been practicing?"

"I'll answer all of your questions tonight if you agree to have dinner with me."

I smiled and waited for his response. I had a few questions of my own.

"It would be my pleasure. What do you have going on right now? Are you going to stick around for the next presentation?"

"No, I have work on my presentation for the discussion tomorrow. I thought I'd focus on some of the questions that came up today. My guess is that you're stuck here, right?"

"Yeah, I'm stuck. I need the continuing education hours."

"Well, have fun and try not to eat too much during the lunch session. I want to take you to this restaurant that I heard about recently. It's supposed to be the bomb if you're into seafood."

"That's what's up. I love seafood. I'm definitely looking forward to a good southern meal."

Damn! His eyes were absolutely piercing and the way he looked at me when he spoke turned the most trivial statements into sensual words.

"Goodbye, Dr. Carlson."

"Goodbye, Alex."

Thankfully, the rest of my day was very busy. I managed to put together a one-hour presentation based on the questions that I received from the morning session. When I was done with the final draft, my excitement started to build. With a glance at the time, I realized I had at a couple of hours to spare before meeting Chris for our dinner date. I located my workout gear and headed over to the gym for a quick work out.

During the thirty minutes of cardio and twenty minutes in the sauna, I thought about my new friend. Naturally, I thought about all of the superficial things that I liked about this strange man, however, his intelligence and ability to hold a meaningful conversation were major pluses. I decided to prepare myself for the potential let down which from experience was sure to come. After all, he couldn't be as perfect as he seemed. This type of man would not be on the market. What if he was married? I hadn't asked, but he hadn't offered up the information either. For some reason, I couldn't remember if he wore a ring or not, which is very unlike me. Usually, it's the first thing I look for on an attractive man. I decided to prepare myself for the remote possibility of marriage. It wouldn't be the first time this vital piece of information was conveniently left out. Over the years, I'd come to realize the importance of lowering your expectations when you meet someone new. In doing so, you're able to circumvent the disappointment that comes when you discover the truth. After my little self-therapy session, I was ready to enjoy my evening with this seemingly perfect man.

I was dressed by six and nervously awaited the phone call from Chris to tell me where to meet him downstairs. Just when I was about to have the desk to ring his room, he called.

"Alex, are you ready?"

He made his inquiry in that dangerously velvety smooth tone.

"Yes and I'm starving. Where are you?"

"Headed downstairs. Meet me at the bar."

"Okay, I'll be there."

Once my heart returned to its normal pace, I took one last look at my appearance and headed downstairs. I wore a proverbial cute little black dress and my favorite black shoes which were stylish and good for dancing. He'd already ordered my favorite drink and nursed a martini while he awaited my arrival. He didn't see me when I entered the room, so I took my time and marveled over his appearance. He was absolutely stunning in his shirt, slacks, and suspenders outfit. No way was this man single, I thought when I finally made it to the bar.

"Dr. Carson, I see you survived day one of the conference."

I laughed and performed a quick ring check. Nothing. Wow.

"Hi, Alex. How was the rest of your day?"

"Productive. I even managed to work in some time at the fitness center."

"Great. So you've worked up your appetite. What was the name of that restaurant? I thought we'd do the taxi thing again. The ride last night was a lot of fun."

"Papadeaux's, and you're right, I've never had so much fun in a taxi especially with a stranger."

We finished our drinks and headed over to the concierge to request a taxi. Within minutes, we were on our way.

The atmosphere in the restaurant was great, and the meal was about as authentic as you could get when it comes to southern cuisine. After dinner, we headed to a local nightspot called Stone Trail. Our waitress was on the money with her suggestion. It was definitely my kind of place. The club was an up-scale little spot that catered to the old school swing out crowd. Some old school music and a man that could make me follow his lead on the dance floor was exactly what I needed to unwind. Initially, I was a little skeptical about my new friend's dancing ability, but to my surprise, he was a swing-out king.

Based primarily on the geographical location, the dance consisted of either six or eight count movements. Whereas the six count movement was most popular in Chicago and other mid-western cities, the eight count movement was more prevalent in the South. With this particular style of dance, masculine leadership is strongly encouraged. In other words, the female's primary role was to follow her leader. When executed in this manner, the presentation was absolutely beautiful. While somewhat accustomed to the southern eight count style of the dance, Chris had to be a native Chicagoan because he killed the six-step. His mastery of the dance was unmistakable and being the consummate follower on the dance floor, I quickly grasped the Chicago style in no time.

The contrast between the two dance styles were relatively subtle, however, the veteran crowd recognized it immediately. They seemed to be impressed by this unfamiliar interpretation of the dance. At one point, we were called to main stage to showcase. Naturally, the ladies were shamelessly checking for Chris. In addition to the number of glares, I received, a few of them were bold enough to step to him for a dance. I was cool with that because I was getting my share of sly winks and dance opportunities from the fellows as well. All in all, this was definitely a night to remember.

We headed for the exit at around three in the morning. We'd both had a fair amount of drinks and felt the effects. However, we were very much aware of our surroundings and the unmistakable attraction that grew by the second. The taxi ride to our hotel was very intense. As soon as the door was closed, I found myself in a passionate kiss that seemed endless. When it was finally over, I literally hyperventilated.

"Alex, we need to talk," Chris said.

I wasn't trying to hear it. I was more interested in continuing the kiss. So was he, but for some reason, he was reluctant.

"Ok, Doctor. What would you like to talk about?"

I sat back with a huff as we approached our hotel. Once inside, we found a secluded little spot on the patio near the pool.

"So, what's on your mind Chris?" I asked to kick-start the conversation.

"Alex, I'm married," he said with an exasperated sigh.

"Really? And, you realized you needed to share this information....when? Now?" I responded sarcastically. "Unbelievable!" I continued.

I was officially done. With everything.

"I'm out."

I left him sitting there and made the long walk to the elevator. Wow. Did I have a sign on my head or did I just look like the kind of woman that would be interested in dating a married man? This was becoming a recurring theme for me. It never failed. Whenever I found myself connecting with someone, they were either married, engaged or shacking. What the hell?

I made it back to my room and immediately started to pack my bags. Thankfully, I was the first speaker for the morning session. I planned to leave as soon as it was over. No sense in hanging around. Talk about Deja vu.

I finished my presentation well within the allotted time, and to my relief, Chris was not there. As luck would have it, I ran into him in the lobby while I waited for my car.

"I guess this is good-by," he said.

He reached for one of the heavier bags that I struggled to carry.

"Yes, it is. You're not here to tell me all about your unfulfilling marriage, are you? If that is the case, you can keep it moving. I'm not interested."

"No, Alex. I've never cheated on my wife, and I don't plan to start now. I just wanted to tell you that I'm sorry if I mislead you. There is just something about you, and I can't explain it. I don't know what kind of brothers you're meeting in DC, but they are seriously slacking."

"Yeah, whatever Chris. I appreciate the kind words, but they serve no purpose here. I'm cool. It is what it is."

"Well, just for the record, I'm not patronizing you to make myself feel better. I meant what I said. If I was single...."

"Save it, Chris."

I stopped him because I did not want to hear the rest. It was always the same.

"It was nice meeting you, but I have to go. I had a lot of fun. I guess I should thank you. You obviously respected me enough to tell me before anything happened. I was digging you just that much. The possibilities were endless."

As the valet turned the corner with my car, I reached up for a quick good-bye kiss on his cheek and retreated to my car. When my bags were securely situated in the trunk, I drove away without looking back. Within the hour, Benz was fastened in his doggy seatbelt, and we were on our way back to DC. At least, I had some new drama to think about during the long drive.

Chapter Fourteen

Sierra

I was relieved to finally make it back to Vegas. In the days following our dinner with Alex, Lenny had become distant, and spoke only when it was absolutely necessary. He was never one to show his emotions or vulnerabilities and up until now, I didn't think he had any. The new Lenny made me feel uneasy because I depended on him to be one step ahead of everything going on around us.

"Lenny, we need to talk," I said one evening after waiting two hours for a john who never showed up.

Come to find out Lenny had given the driver the wrong location. This was unprecedented.

"About what, Sierra?" he asked.

He clearly was not in the mood for conversation.

"Lenny, what happened today has never happened before and I'm worried about you. Janell and some of the other girls are worried too."

Waiting for a response, which never came, I continued.

"I know that you have a lot on your mind, but we depend on you. It just seems like you're slowly pulling away from us."

"You're right Sierra, I have a lot on my mind. I'm finding it hard to accept the fact that Tiffany is really gone. In a way, I feel responsible for what happened to her because of the way I handled her back in college."

Finally, I thought, he's opening up about it. Maybe he's ready to move forward.

"I never forgave her for killing my child, but I never stopped loving her. If only I could have swallowed my pride, we could have made it work."

His words cut through me like a knife. I was already aware of his feelings but to hear him say it, only made it worse. At that moment I almost told him that I loved him, but I didn't think he could handle it right now. I had to find a way to get him past the grief which was destroying him right before my eyes. Suddenly, it came to me.

"Lenny, why don't you call Alex? You need to deal with this before it destroys you."

I banked on the fact that Tiffany might have said something in the letter that would allow him to move on. It was a huge risk but it was one that I was willing to take.

"I think you're right, Sierra. I've put it off long enough."

I called Alex the next day and worked out the details. Lenny would meet her in Alabama the following week and although I was strongly opposed, he would be going alone. Technically, Lenny was not my man, but I was in love with him. Everyone seemed to know it except Lenny. My long term goal was to exit the business as his wife and live happily ever after, but there was one problem. I couldn't have kids, and I knew Lenny wanted a family. I had purposely avoided telling him about my hysterectomy because I believed that once he fell in love with me it wouldn't matter. I just had to be patient a little while longer.

Alex

I made it back to DC in record time and was eager to get back to work. As the newest senior partner for the firm, I had to carry my weight. This would be easy since work was the only thing going on in my life anyway. The only other highlight in my life was the phone call from Lawrence. He wanted to see me again. I was surprised because the last visit had taken place less than a month ago.

It was around noon when I got the call from Sierra. I had actually expected it much sooner. During my brief encounter with Lenny, I suspected his tough exterior was only a façade. According to Tiffany, Lenny was extremely sensitive.

Tiffany also told me about Lenny's extra-curricular activities during his college days. However, I could have sworn that she told me that he went legit after graduation and made a clean exit from his life of crime. Now, I wasn't so sure. There was something really shady about him, and I was hoping to find out during our visit. There was also the confusion regarding his relationship with Sierra. Were they a couple or was he merely her pimp? For obvious reasons, I was concerned about Sierra's health. After all, there was a remote possibility that Lenny could have contracted the disease from Tiffany or vice versa. However, since neither Sierra nor Lenny seemed to be concerned, I assumed they were both okay.

It was just too much to try and understand at one time I thought while I called my travel agent to make reservations for my trip to Alabama. I planned to get to the bottom of it once and for all during this trip.

Chapter Fifteen

Alex

As the plane touched down at the airport in Tuskegee, Lenny felt a huge lump in his throat. He still couldn't believe Tiffany was gone and he was apprehensive about what she had to say in the letter. Did she blame him? Had he been too hard on her after the abortion? If only he could go back. There were so many things he would have done differently, and so many things that he wanted to say to her.

Alex was first in the long line of onlookers when Lenny exited the corridor of the runway. At first glance, he wasn't sure if it was her, but she was the only person that waved to him and called his name. This girl was absolutely gorgeous, which for some reason he failed to notice when they first met.

"Alex, how are you? I want to thank you for taking the time to do this for me. It really means a lot to me," Lenny said while he gave me a hug and a kiss on the cheek.

I had to take a step back as a warm familiar feeling entered my body and my nipples grew firm under my bra. What the hell was that all about? How could I be attracted to Tiffany's ex-boyfriend and a man who might very well be my cousin's pimp?

"Hi, Lenny. There's no need to thank me. I'm just glad I could do this for you and Tiffany. In case you were wondering, I want to assure you that I still haven't read your letter and I don't want you to feel obligated to discuss the contents with me. I know this is hard for you, so if you need to talk, I will listen."

Lenny remained silent as Alex took charge of the situation.

"Let's go," she said and motioned toward the baggage claim.

From there, she quickly located the rental car that she picked up the day before and they drove to Tiffany's mother's house.

"Lenny, before we head over to the cemetery, I thought you might want to say hello to the Robinsons. I told them we would be in town to visit Tiffany's grave, and they really want to see you," I suggested cautiously.

I braced myself for his response. I decided not to tell him until we were in route for fear he might object.

"That's cool Alex, I have a few things I want to say to them as well. Her mom was always nice to me. I can only imagine how hard this must be for her. Tiffany was her only child."

I was both shocked and relieved by his response.

As we turned into the driveway of Tiffany's house, a sense of calm came over me. All of a sudden, I knew the visit would produce a positive outcome. Before I could ring the doorbell, Mrs. Robinson opened the door and greeted us with a smile. Mr. Robinson stood behind her with a hand placed firmly about her waist symbolizing his role as protector. Tiffany probably saw in Lenny the same characteristics that she saw in her father.

Tiffany's home was immaculate with hard wood floors and ceramic tile everywhere. The first time I visited her home, I was even more puzzled about Tiffany's decision to sell her body because her parents appeared to be more than capable to give her anything she wanted or needed. It just didn't make any sense. We went into the kitchen which was enormous and equipped with all the latest appliances. We sat down at the table while Mrs. Robinson made coffee, and the two men were engaged in a little small talk. It was nothing like I expected. No tension whatsoever. When Mrs. Robinson finished serving the coffee, she immediately started the dialogue about Tiffany.

"Lenny, I want you to know that Tiffany loved you very much. When the two of you broke up, Henry and I were totally surprised."

Lenny knew better than to interrupt. He just sat back and listened.

"When she came home for semester break, I suspected that she was pregnant. A mother always knows."

Mrs. Robinson smiled.

"I shared my thoughts with my husband."

She paused and took a sip of her coffee.

"He was ready to come looking for you with a shotgun."

She chuckled and looked over at Mr. Robinson who was thoroughly embarrassed.

"I told Henry to just wait and see how the two of you would handle the situation. When it was time for her to go back to school, she still hadn't told us. So, I thought maybe I had been mistaken."

Lenny tried to interject, but she held up her hand and continued.

"A couple of days after she returned to school, she called to tell me that the two of you had broken up and that she didn't want to be in school anymore. I asked her what happened, but she never really told me. I convinced her to stay in school, but she was never the same after that. She stopped coming home and rarely returned our calls. We didn't know what to do. At the end of the semester, she had straight 'A's, so, we assumed she was okay and just wanted some space."

After a moment of reflection she continued.

"The change in her behavior continued up until she graduated and then out of the blue, she informed us of her plan to join the Army. Henry and I didn't like it, but we decided not to make a fuss about it. We were just happy that she had a plan for her future. Of course you know what happened after that."

She looked at Lenny and me with tears in her eyes.

"She was here with us for a whole month after the graduation, and she was so happy. I thought we had our little girl back. When she left for Colorado, we thought she would be gone for at least a month before she could come home for a visit, however, she called me that following week to tell me that she was on her way home. She wouldn't discuss it over the phone, but I knew that something was wrong. The next day she walked into the house, sat us down, and told us that she was HIV positive. She said that it was likely that she got it from a needle stick during her training in nursing school. We were devastated, of course, but we were determined to do whatever we could to keep her alive. She educated herself about the disease and did all of the things she needed to do to stay alive until about a year ago when she just gave up. That's when she told me about the pregnancy. She told me how you wanted to do the right thing, Lenny, and how hurt you were when she told you what she had done. We cried together for what seemed like forever. Then, I told her about my suspicions when she came home that semester. I asked her if she did it because she was afraid of how Henry and I would have reacted, or if she did it because she just wasn't ready to be a mother. She never really answered me, so I don't know why she did it Lenny. I guess that was my main reason for wanting to talk to you. Can you please tell us what happened? Why did she think that she couldn't come to us?"

"I don't know, Mrs. Robinson. I wanted to come and tell you in person. I wanted to assure you of my plans take care of Tiffany and the baby, but she wouldn't let me. She kept telling me that she wanted to do it herself and against my better judgment, I allowed her to do things her way. I have racked my brain to understand why she did it, but I still don't have any answers. I just know that it was completely out of character for her. She loved children."

Mr. Robinson had been quiet up until that point, but he finally spoke.

"Lenny, we have a point of reference for when our daughter changed, but we are frustrated because we don't know what happened to make her change so drastically. She told us over and over not to blame ourselves, but it's hard. I need to know if there was something that we did to make our daughter so unhappy".

Lenny thought about it for a moment and answered the question as honestly as he could.

"No, Mr. Robinson, she loved you both, and she knew that you loved her."

Mr. Robinson let out a sigh of relief and grabbed Mrs. Robinson's hand.

"Thank you Lenny," he said and reached over to shake Lenny's hand.

I decided it was time for us to go. I was sure that the Robinson's needed some time alone. Dusk approached as we left, so I asked Lenny if he would be okay to visit the cemetery the next day. He agreed and suggested we grab some dinner before going to the hotel. We found a nice Italian restaurant near the hotel which turned out to be an excellent choice. The food was great. Lenny and I ate in comfortable silence which gave us time to process everything that was going on. At the hotel, we decided to have a much needed drink at the bar before we retired for the night. After our first drink, we were able to relax and engage in a little conversation.

"Lenny, please don't take this the wrong way, but I need to clarify a few things. Tiffany told me about your entrepreneurial activities back in college."

I started my little speech cautiously not wanting to sound accusatory.

Lenny smiled.

"Is that so?" he asked mischievously.

"Well, would you care to elaborate?"

"Only if you can tell me the source of your curiosity."

"Hmm, the source of my curiosity," I repeated. "Let me just confirm for the record that I am curious, very curious as a matter of fact."

"Why are you curious, Alex?" he asked.

He leaned forward and looked directly into my eyes. He was close enough for me to smell the Hennessy on his breath and feel the air that came out of his nose each time he exhaled.

I knew I was treading in dangerous water with this man. I was definitely attracted to him, but he was completely off limits on so many levels and for so many reasons.

"Lenny, I think we need to leave now."

My hoarse tone completely gave me away.

"I totally agree," he said

He touched my chin and forced me to look at him. Without looking at the check, he placed a hundred dollar bill on the table, reached for my hand, and escorted me to the hotel lobby. I decided to leave him to the task of obtaining his room key. I needed to get away from him immediately, but when I turned to leave, I felt his hand on my elbow.

"Alex, wait, let me see you to your room."

"Lenny, I don't think that's such a good idea. I'll be okay, I promise."

Before I knew it, Lenny had his room key, and we were standing in the elevator.

"Alex, I'm not going to comment on what just happened at the bar or what happened at the airport or what happened during the drive over here."

Damn, he noticed my nipples at the airport, I thought. It wasn't an accident either when he touched my thigh during the drive over here.

"We're adults, and we have adult imaginations. You're very beautiful, Alex, and I have a passion for beautiful things. However, it doesn't mean I want to get you into my bed. Contrary to what you might believe, I'm not the person that you think I am. Good night, Alex."

"Good night Lenny," I said softly and turned to enter my room.

"Lenny, wait! I need to give you the letter."

For the briefest time, Lenny had forgotten about the letter. He retraced his steps and followed Alex into her room. Alex wasted no time and quickly handed the worn envelope over to Lenny. She felt like a weight had been lifted from her shoulders. He held the letter in the palm of his hand for a moment, and then looked at Alex. What she saw was raw emotion and realized he should not be left alone to read the letter.

"Lenny, I'm going to take a shower and do some work before I go to sleep. Have a seat and open the letter. If you want to talk, I'm here."

I left Lenny on the sofa in the adjoining room. I took a shower and attempted to read over some files before I went to bed, however, I couldn't focus my attention away from the events of the day. Where was all of this going? Why was I so attracted to Lenny? Was the drama ever going to end?

Just as I started to drift off to sleep, I heard a soft tap at my door. I was startled at first, but then I realized it was Lenny.

"Yes Lenny, what is it?"

I scrambled up to find my robe.

"Alex, we need to talk."

"Okay, I'll be right out."

I found my robe and rushed into the next room. Lenny paced back and forth like a caged animal.

"Alex, this is not good."

He spoke through clenched teeth.

"What is it Lenny?"

"Read it!" he said fiercely.

He shoved the letter into my hands. I hesitated for a moment to decide if it was the right thing to do. After all, if Tiffany had wanted me to read the letter, she would have told me. However, judging by Lenny's reaction I didn't have a choice. I took the letter, sat down on the sofa and slowly began to read.

Dear Lenny,

Chances are you will never read this letter, for obvious reasons. My therapist suggested writing the letter because she thought it might be good for me. First, I need to tell you that I love you more than I've ever loved anyone or anything in my life, and I know that you loved me just as much. Believe it or not, memories of you and your love for me have sustained me to this point and have been a constant source of strength.

Looking back, my decision regarding the baby changed our lives forever. I have carried your pain, as well as my own, for all of these years and will continue to do so until the day I die. I need you to know I wanted to have your child, Lenny - your child. The thing is, I wasn't sure if the baby that I carried was actually your child. I want you to know that I never cheated on you, never even thought about it.

Carlos gave me a ride back to the dorm after a party one night. A party that you didn't want me to attend. You went home that weekend and out of frustration about being alone, I went anyway. Once I got there, I quickly realized I'd made a mistake and I just wanted to get back to the dorm. I ran into Carlos outside the club, and he offered me a ride which I gladly accepted. However, he didn't take me to the dorm as he had promised, and I'm convinced he never intended to. Instead, he took me down the deserted road near campus, and he raped me. I begged him to stop, and when he didn't, I threatened to tell you. He laughed at me and reminded me that I'd broken my promise to you about going to the party. I didn't know what to do. I was paralyzed with grief and guilt. In the end, I decided not to tell you. I just pretended that it never happened, and I avoided Carlos as much as I could. A few weeks later, I discovered that I was pregnant. I wanted to have your baby more than anything in the world, but I couldn't take the chance. What if Carlos was the father? I didn't know if I could love a child that was conceived through such evil. I counted the days over and over again, but there was no way for me to be sure. When I went home for the winter break, I had the abortion. I knew you would be angry at first, but I thought you would eventually forgive me and that we would just move on. Obviously, it didn't happen that way and when you broke up with me, I honestly felt like my life had ended. Along with the guilt and the shame that seemed to weigh me down more and more as the days went by, I had to deal with the fact that you had moved on. It nearly killed me to see you with other girls, but the way that you treated me was the part that literally broke my spirit. It was as if I never existed...

As for my parents, I avoided them as much as possible for fear that my mother would instinctively discover my secret. Funny thing is, she already knew.

To make a long story short, Lenny, I was lost without you. I grew to hate myself, and I was convinced that no man would ever love me the way that you did. It was the self-hatred that led me to the place where I am today. If you recall, I no longer had a dorm room when I returned that semester. I couldn't ask my parents for the money because I didn't want them to know about my living arrangements. I started out stripping just to earn a little extra money to pay for my apartment off campus. It didn't take long for me to get caught up in the money, the clothes, and of course, the attention. I began to measure my self-worth by the amount of money I made and the attention that I got. It was definitely an ego booster, but it only lasted while I was on stage. Once the lights came on, reality would set in and the self-hatred would take over again.

One night, the owner of the club noticed my solemn demeanor and decided I needed a little "something to help me get by." He took me into a back room where some of the other girls hung out. There were all types of drugs lying around, and I didn't know one from the other. I tried all of them. Heroin was the last one. Because of all the other stuff I'd already taken, I had no problem being injected with a needle. Of course, he was more than willing to do it for me. I remember one of the girls tried to stop me. She said it would ruin my life, but I didn't listen. After one hit, I was hooked. All of a sudden, I felt no pain, no sadness, and no regret. I thought I'd found the solution to all of my problems. It was weekends only at first. I kept thinking I could control the drug. However, the drug had control of me from day one. Before I knew it, I had a serious habit, which was impossible to maintain by just taking my clothes off on the weekends. I needed money, so I took the elevator up or down, depending on how you want to look at it, and moved on to the next level of degradation. I started selling my body.

The heroin took away the pain that I felt over losing you and the guilt that I felt about the baby, but I was not prepared for the consequences. For one year, I shot heroin every day, however, I never missed a class. No one, not even my closest friends, knew that I was a junky prostitute.

Somehow, I found the strength to get clean. I checked myself into a cheap hotel all alone except for my friend, Tracy, one of the girls from the club. I considered going to a detox center, but I was too proud to ask for help or to discuss my problems with complete strangers. Not to mention, I didn't want the risk of having my parents find out. By the grace of God, I got through the withdrawal phase. There were times when I thought I was dying, and I actually considered taking my own life. It took me three weeks to get clean and that experience alone helped me resist the urge to ever use again.

I left the hotel on a Friday, two days before the start of the fall semester. I'd managed to avoid my parents all summer by telling them that I was in Mexico on a student exchange program. I bought myself a few more weeks by telling them that I got a part time job and couldn't visit before classes started. I hated to lie, but I couldn't let them see me in that condition. In addition to the fact that I had lost thirty pounds, the track marks were disgusting. I couldn't come up with a good enough story to explain the long sleeved shirts in August.

Somehow, I made it through nursing school and joined the Army. That was how I found out that I was HIV positive. I was absolutely devastated, but I was convinced that it was God's way of punishing me for my sins. It took me some time, but I finally accepted my fate. For a while, I was functional. I did everything the doctors told me to do. I had to take fifteen to twenty pills a day, but I was healthy. I became a counselor at the county clinic and developed an AIDS prevention program for the public school system. It wasn't much, but it paid the bills. I also felt like I was actually making a difference.

My doctors warned me that at some point, the medication could stop working. When it happened, I was not prepared. I had five good years with no symptoms of the virus. Then all of a sudden, I was at death's door. The doctors were hopeful that a new drug combination was on the horizon, but nothing really worked. To make matters worse, the new drugs made me feel far worse than the disease ever did. Eventually, I stopped taking the pills and started preparing for the completion of my journey. I've asked myself if what I was doing was selfish or if I should keep fighting for my parents' sake. I just can't find any good reason to keep fighting this losing battle. My father is the strongest man I know, but he's powerless. My mom is a praying woman, but she is slowly losing her faith. I can't allow this disease to destroy all of us. It is time for me to end our suffering.

I've asked God to forgive me for my sins. My only wish now is that you can forgive me. I love you, Lenny.
Tiffany

This was absolutely devastating. I had no idea Tiffany was dealing with so many issues. I was also a little hurt that she didn't confide in me, but on the other hand, I understood.

Lenny was a mad man and hardly able to control his anger. He was on the cell phone frantically dialing numbers and threatening anyone who refused to give him the information that he desperately needed. After a couple of hours, he finally found someone who could tell him what he needed to know. Ramon, the club owner, was apparently in jail doing life as a repeat offender for drug trafficking. However, Carlos, Lenny's best friend in college, actually answered the phone at two a.m. Now a born again minister, husband, and father, Carlos tearfully admitted to the horrible act and apologized for the pain and suffering that he caused Tiffany.

"Lenny, man, I'm sorry. I didn't mean for it to happen. I was drunk and high. I didn't know what I was doing until it was too late. I have agonized over this since the day it happened, and I have never been able to forgive myself. I'm responsible for all of this. I took her life."

At this point, Lenny was in tears and so was I. It was just too much to handle. He finally hung up the phone without saying goodbye to Carlos and fell asleep on the sofa with his head on my lap. I'm not sure how or when I went to sleep, but I woke up to find myself wrapped in Lenny's arms.

As I lay in the dark and listened to Lenny's heartbeat, he startled me.

"Alex, I did this to her."

I tried to sit up so that I could look at him, but he wouldn't let me move.

"Lenny, you can't do this. You can't blame yourself. It'll destroy you."

"I was not there when she needed me," Lenny said with his voice barely above a whisper, "and I said some horrible things to her that night when she told me about the abortion."

I remained silent with the sense that he needed to talk. I just needed to shut up and listen.

"And Carlos. He was my best friend, my right hand man, and partner in crime. How could he betray me like that and continue to break bread with me? What was going through his mind when he...."

He couldn't bring himself to say the words. It was much too painful.

"I want to kill him, Alex. I want him to feel the pain that he caused Tiffany and I want him to suffer the way that Tiffany suffered."

I could hear his heart speed up as his anger continued to grow, but still, I said nothing. I just listened.

"I should have known something was wrong when Tiffany started giving Carlos the cold shoulder, but I just thought she resented him because we were so close."

"Lenny you didn't know. I need you to think about this. I mean really think about it. If you didn't know these things were happening, how could you be responsible? I'm a firm believer that everything happens for a reason. I don't know the reason and neither do you. The fact is, we may never know. Tiffany is gone and you can't change that, but you have to find a way to live with the circumstances."

All of a sudden, he grew quiet, but he held me closer as his mind traveled backwards. He was probably unaware of the fact that he was softly caressing my shoulder and that my heart now beat as rapidly as his. I was unraveling both emotionally and physically. When I couldn't stand it any longer, I decided to run.

"Lenny, I think it's time for me to go back to the other room. We both need to get some sleep. We have a long day ahead of us tomorrow. The cemetery is located just over an hour away, and I was hoping to get an early start."

"Alex, don't go."

"But Lenny, I…."

I tried to tell him my reasons for wanting to leave, but he refused to listen.

"I already know what you're thinking and what you're feeling because I'm feeling it too. I don't want to complicate things any more than you do, and I won't pretend to understand what is happening between us. I just know that I need you here with me right now."

In the darkness of the room, I tried to see his eyes and his facial expressions in order to gauge his sincerity, but it was useless.

"Okay Lenny, I'll stay with you," I said with a sigh and gave in to his wishes.

"Thank you Alex."

Sierra

I hadn't heard a word from Lenny since he boarded the plane the previous day. It was my fifth call to his cell phone that morning and still no answer. I was a little concerned at first, but now, I was in panic mode. My mind was all over the place. I took in a deep breath and held it to make sure that the weed saturated my lungs completely. Lenny left me with a hefty supply, but at the rate I was going, it would be gone by the end of the day. Something was going on in Alabama. I could just feel it.

Had it not been for the fact that Lenny left me in charge, I probably would have remained in bed for the rest of the day. However, I had seventeen girls to look after and it was not going to be an easy task. I dragged myself out of bed, took a shower, and made a pot of coffee. My first order of business was to review the number of requests that we had for the day and the number of ladies that were available. The next step was to arrange their schedules to accommodate as many customers as we could. Once that was done, I contacted the girls and the drivers and gave them the itinerary for the day. In all, it took me about two hours to complete a task that Lenny would have completed in thirty minutes.

It was noon, and I still hadn't heard from Lenny. Just as I was about to pick up the phone to call him again, my phone rang. It was Lenny.

"Lenny, what is going on? I've called you a million times. Is everything okay?"

I tried to stay cool, however, I wasn't doing a very good job.

"Everything is okay. I'm just trying to sort through all the details," he responded quietly.

"Well what did you find out? Did you read the letter?"

I couldn't stand the suspense. I needed to know if this trip was going to help Lenny to move on.

"Sierra, I don't want to go into any details right now. We'll talk when I get back."

"But, Lenny…"

"Sierra, let it go. We'll talk when I get back. How are things going? Have you had any problems?"

"Everything is okay. Just hurry back," I said.

The feeling of being totally let down crept through me.

"I will. I'll call you tonight."

"Okay, I'll be waiting."

The sound of the click on the other end of the phone was deafening. I forgot to ask him when he was coming home.

Latrice

"Keith! Please say something! Open your eyes!"

Keith's sister frantically tried to get a response from her dying brother, but from where I was stood, it seemed hopeless. It happened so fast. One minute, he was talking to Arlissa, Yasmin's 8-year-old daughter, and now he was lying on the ground in a pool of his own blood. Yasmin sat in the back of a police car with a dazed look on her face, and everyone else was silent as the paramedics worked to save Keith's life.

This was bound to happen. Keith had managed to ruin the lives of so many people, yet he continued to walk around and act like a saint.

"Latrice, what happened?"

In between sobs, my grandmother desperately tried to make sense of what had just happened.

"Granny, you know why she did it. Someone should have put a bullet in his ass a long time ago."

I couldn't hold my tongue any longer. I was tired of pretending and tired of lying about Keith.

"She shot him because she thought he was messing with her daughter."

After all these years I finally made a statement about Keith, and I felt nothing but relief.

"Keith is a pervert and you know it! Everyone around here knows it!"

I screamed to the top of my voice.

"Latrice, stop that foolishness. She didn't have to shoot that boy, he wasn't bothering nobody," my grandmother hissed.

By now, the ambulance was gone to the hospital with Keith hanging on by a thread. There were close to fifty people standing in the yard, and my grandmother still tried to protect his image just as she did when Sierra made her confession almost twenty years ago. This time, I was not going to stand for it. It was time for everyone to hear the truth.

"Latrice, please tell me he didn't do anything to Arlissa," Yori sobbed on the other end of the phone.

Someone must have called her and gave me the phone. I placed her on speaker so that everyone could hear what she had to say.

"All I know is, Yasmin drove up and saw Keith outside talking to Arlissa, and she snapped. She jumped out of the car, ran up to Keith, and started shooting."

"Where is Arlissa? I need to talk to her."

Yori wanted to make sure that her niece was okay.

"I made her go in the house," my grandmother said with a serious attitude.

From the tone of her voice, I could see where this was going. Arlissa, an eight year old would be blamed for what happened. My God, I thought as I headed toward my favorite hangout. This family is totally messed up.

"I'm on my way," Yori said and hung up the phone. Keith was pronounced dead on arrival.

Chapter Sixteen

Alex

I was supposed to meet Lenny in the hotel lobby in five minutes, and I was a complete wreck. I was stressed over the events from last night and over the task that we had before us. In light of his volatile display of emotion regarding Tiffany's letter, I was unsure about Lenny's state of mind. I tried to prepare myself for every possible reaction.

I took one last peep in the mirror and headed to the door. I was not completely happy with my appearance. Although I had taken a little extra time to conceal the bags that were under my eyes from lack of sleep, they were still very visible. I wore a pair of loose fitting black pants with a cute little black top. My hair was pulled back in a ponytail and at the last minute, I removed my contacts and wore my glasses instead. I was trying desperately to down play my personal attributes. My goal was to end this trip with my dignity intact and my conscience clear.

I spotted Lenny as soon as I entered the lobby. He was on his cell phone talking to Sierra most likely. When I approached, he quickly ended the conversation and slowly made his way toward me. Once again, I was taken aback by his overwhelming good looks. The black pants and soft cotton shirt that he wore must have been made especially for him. There was a subtle sexiness in the way his pants dropped right below his waist and how the close fit of his shirt revealed the tight ripples that were permanently etched into his abdomen. Physically, everything about him was perfect and confidence seemed to pour out of him with every stride as he came closer to me. The way that he walked and his swagger implied that he owned the building. At the same time, he seemed to be completely unaware of the curious stares that came at him from every direction. He was definitely a head turner.

"Good morning Alex," he said softly.

He checked me out from head to toe.

"Did you manage to get any sleep last night?"

"I think I got a couple of hours, but I definitely could have used more," I said sheepishly, wondering if he'd noticed my bags.

All of a sudden, I felt naked as the intensity of Lenny's inspection increased.

"How are you doing?"

"I'm hanging in, I suppose. Are you hungry? We can grab a late breakfast if you like, but I don't have much of an appetite," Lenny offered when his assessment came to an end.

"No, I'm okay. We should probably get going since we're already behind schedule."

I glanced at my Rolex. It was quickly approaching noon, and we were both scheduled to leave later that night.

"Alright, pretty lady. After you," he said and made a gesture toward the nearest exit.

"Lenny, if you don't mind, could you drive?"

"Of course" he said reaching for the keys, "you're not planning to go to sleep on me, are you?"

"No, I wouldn't do that. I just think you should drive."

"Because I'm a man?" he asked with a small grin.

"Pretty much," I said shortly.

I chose not to elaborate on the issue and made a mental note to avoid all things that pertained to gender roles and relationships.

We made the seventy-two mile trip in record time it seemed. We kept the conversation light and talked about topics that were safe: the weather, politics and sports. Half way into the trip, we got into a heated discussion about Kobe Bryant.

"Alex, he's the best player in the league right now. The dude is off the chain," Lenny argued.

He seemed thoroughly surprised by my opinion about the athlete.

"You're right, he's very talented, but here's the deal. Kobe gets no love from me because he's a cry baby! And until he wins a championship *without* Shaq, he will always have something to prove to me."

"And another thing, I get tired of the media always comparing Kobe to Jordan. To me, there is no comparison. First of all, Kobe got picked up by a team that already had the tools to win a championship, a dominating center. Who couldn't win a championship with Shaquille O'Neal? Jordan, on the other hand, had Bill Cartwright. Bill Cartwright!"

I repeated the name for emphasis to get my point across.

"So, Jordan spent his first few years in the league trying to build a championship team from the ground up. All Kobe had to do was go along for the ride."

By now, Lenny was in tears with laughter, thoroughly amused by my animated commentary.

"You're really serious about this, aren't you?"

"Absolutely."

Nothing could get me going like the Kobe versus Jordan debate.

"Wow," he said when he finally gained his composure. "Don't take this the wrong way, Alex. I'm just surprised. You don't seem like the typical sports fanatic."

Just when I was about to respond, I looked up and saw the sign. We were less than five minutes away from our destination. We were both silent while we traveled down the deserted, gravel point road. Lenny parked the car, and with both hands on the steering wheel and his head resting on the seat, he examined our surroundings. Not wanting to make the first move I remained silent to give Lenny a chance to organize his feelings.

"So this is it," he said softly. "Where is she, Alex?"

I took out the slip of paper that Mrs. Robinson had given me with the plot number and location.

"Follow me."

I reached for his hand and led him to Tiffany's grave.

As we walked the lonely path, the surroundings became familiar. I stopped in my tracks and released Lenny's hand. Directly in front of us stood an exquisitely designed tombstone which was complete with Tiffany's date of birth, earthly departure and epitaph: "To live is Christ, and to die is gain..." Philippians 1:21.

For a brief moment, Lenny stood still seemingly paralyzed with grief. The intensity of which was written all over his face. Finally, he kneeled down and began to trace the letters of her name with his fingers. I felt completely powerless and unsure of my role. After all, we were virtual strangers and under such tragic circumstances, was I supposed to offer words of comfort or simply leave him alone? Ultimately, my instincts took over and before I knew it, I knelt beside him.

"It's okay to cry, Lenny...." I whispered softly in his ear.

Almost immediately, the tears began to flow like a stream. I imagined his tears represented a mixture of feelings to include guilt, regret, loss, and above all—love. Without a doubt, he never stopped loving her. I never got a chance to discuss all of the dynamics of her relationship with Lenny, but I knew that Tiffany was still in love with Lenny up to the very end. The entire situation was very disturbing. I thought love was supposed to conquer all.

Chapter Seventeen

Latrice

Yasmin was charged with first-degree murder, and quite naturally the family was evenly divided over the issue of justification. Was she provoked? Had Keith finally done something to push her over the edge? I was still in shock over the fact that Keith was really dead, however, I was not surprised. Yasmin only did what Sierra, Alex, and I often dreamed of doing and under the right circumstances, it could have been either one of us. According to Yori, it was just as I had suspected. Yasmin snapped when she saw Keith talking to her daughter—alone. To me, it seemed like an open and shut case, a crime of passion.

Two days had passed since the horrible incident and I still hadn't been able to reach Sierra or Alex. I wanted to help Yasmin, but I was sure that a statement from me would probably fall on deaf ears. However, if the three of us could do it together, the prosecutor might be inclined to drop the charges or at least offer a deal. In the meanwhile, Yasmin was slowly losing touch with reality while she sat in jail and recounted that day over and over in her mind and to anyone else who would listen.

"I just wanted him to stay away from my daughter, that's all I wanted Latrice," she repeated continuously during one of our phone conversations.

At the rate that she was going, the insanity defense was becoming a very viable option. Where the hell was Alex when we needed her?

After dialing Sierra's cell phone non-stop for over an hour, she finally answered. Not bothering to find out why she hadn't answered or returned my previous calls, I got straight to the point.

"Sierra, Keith is dead. Yasmin shot him and she's in jail for first degree murder."

"Latrice, slow down and tell me what the hell is going on!" Sierra yelled.

I took a deep breath and repeated what I had just said.

"She killed him, Sierra, and we have to do something or she's going to jail for killing that bastard," I whispered.

My throat tightened as I fought to hold back the tears.

"You're right, Latrice, we have to help her. I'm on my way home first thing in the morning".

"I can't get in touch with Alex. She's not answering her phone either. We need to get her here as soon as possible. Hell, she's probably going to have to defend Yasmin. I'm sure she won't be able to afford a decent lawyer."

"Don't worry. I know how to reach her. We'll be there," Sierra said with confidence.

I wasn't sure how or why she thought that she would be able to reach Alex when no one else could. I was just relieved that Sierra was willing to help. God knows she had every reason to turn her back on the situation after the way the family handled her when she tried to expose Keith.

Damn. I forgot to tell her that Granny was in the hospital. The events of the day must have gotten the best of her. She had a seizure shortly after Keith was pronounced dead, but she seemed to be doing well. Chances were she would be released before Alex and Sierra made it home. No sense in giving them something else to worry about on the way.

After I ended my conversation with Sierra, I promptly broke down in tears. I cried for Yasmin and Yori, for Sierra, for Alex and myself. I cried for all the things that we'd already endured and the things that were to come. I knew at some point we would have to deal with the past, but it never occurred to me that it would happen like this.

Sierra

When my tears were finally gone, I picked up the phone to call Lenny so that I could break the news to Alex. As I dialed the number, I realized I no longer had a choice as to whether or not to tell Lenny about my past.

"Lenny, I have to talk to Alex."

I was prepared to leave a message since Lenny rarely answered his phone when I called.

"Is everything okay Sierra?" Lenny asked.

"No, not really. We have a bit of a family emergency, and we need to get home as soon as possible. I'll explain everything later. I really need to talk to Alex".

"Sierra, what's wrong? Is everything ok?"

Alex was alarmed like I knew she would be. I quickly confirmed her fears about the reason for the call.

"No, everything is not okay, Alex. It's Keith. He's dead. Yasmin killed him," I said bluntly.

"Sierra what happened? Did he do something to her?"

Alex had to sit down. She reeled as her mind raced back to the time in her life that she wanted so desperately to forget. A time when she actually fantasized about doing what Yasmin had actually done. Instantly, she knew something must have triggered Yasmin's actions. What had he done?

"What did he do, Sierra?"

"Apparently, Yasmin went to pick Arlissa up from Granny's when she saw Keith standing outside talking to her - alone. She jumped out of the car with her boyfriend's gun and shot him. Alex, I'm leaving tomorrow morning. Can you meet me there? We have to tell the police what happened to us."

"Of course, I will be there. I'm on the first thing out of here in the morning. Does she have an attorney?" Alex wanted to know.

"I'm pretty sure that she doesn't, so are you licensed to practice in Louisiana?"

"Yes."

For the first time ever, Alex was thankful for obtaining a license in one of the most complex states in the union.

"We'll figure it out tomorrow, Sierra. Have you discussed any of this with Lenny?"

Alex asked in a hushed voice so that Lenny couldn't hear.

"No, not everything. Is he still there?"

"Yes. Lenny, it's for you."

Alex passed the receiver to Lenny and retreated to the bathroom. She sat on the floor, covered her face with both hands, and willed herself not to cry. So, this is how it was going to play out? Finally, the family would know their horrible secret. What would her mother and father think about her? Would they blame her as Sierra's mother had so many years ago?

Sierra

"Lenny, there's something I've been meaning to tell you for a long time. I told you a few things about my childhood, but I left some things out. When I was a little girl, I was molested and raped by an older cousin. It started when I was around four, and it continued well into my teens. Latrice and Alex were molested as well, but my experience was far worse. When I was nineteen, I told my mom and she blamed me for everything.

By that time, I was in tears.

"Because of this, I left everything - my kids, my family…..everything."

Lenny was not surprised by the revelation. He always sensed something horrible happened to her. He'd been around long enough to know the signs of an abused woman, and Sierra had all the traits.

"I'm telling you now because the bastard is dead. One of my younger cousins killed him. She's in jail, and we have to go home."

Sierra's words were barely intelligible as a result of her uncontrollable sobs.

"Sierra, I'm coming too. Pull yourself together, and I will meet you there tomorrow. We'll do whatever we have to do to help your cousin. And Sierra, I want you to stop blaming yourself for what happened. You were just a kid. I need you to hear me. It wasn't your fault, okay. Are you listening?"

"Yes," Sierra whispered.

"Get some rest. We will talk in the morning."

"Thanks, Lenny. Goodbye."

When Alex finally exited the bathroom, she found Lenny waiting patiently on the sofa. Since leaving the cemetery, she and Lenny had not exchanged many words. Instead the two had comforted each other in silence with both being lost in their individual thoughts.

"Alex, Sierra told me about your family's ordeal, and my heart aches for all of you."

"Thanks Lenny."

At that moment, I completely lost my composure. I cried nonstop for what seemed like an eternity. Lenny simply held me until all of the tears were gone. Like the night before, we slept on the sofa. Only this time, he consoled me.

Chapter Eighteen

Alex

To my surprise, we were greeted at the airport by Sierra, her mom, and two of my aunts. As Lenny raced to the car rental place, Sierra and I retrieved our luggage.

"Alex, Granny's in the hospital. She had a seizure shortly after she got the news about Keith. She was doing ok until this morning, now, she's unresponsive. The doctor is saying something about brain damage."

Sierra was visibly shaken as she gave me the news.

While I was upset about not being told before now, I decided to let it go.

"What hospital is she in?"

I was already thinking about the potential reasons for her sudden decline and eager to hear the physician's rationale. I had to remain calm for my family. If I lost it, everyone else would as well.

"Southwestern," Sierra said hesitantly.

"You gotta be kidding me. Whose idea was it to take her there?" I asked, unable to contain my annoyance.

My family was well aware of my opinion regarding that particular hospital. As a medical malpractice attorney, I was astonished over the outrageous number of wrongful death cases associated with the facility. The place was a breeding ground for incompetence. I'd warned my family about it many times and made it perfectly clear that if anything ever happened to Granny, she would be taken to one of the other hospitals in town.

"My mom rode in the ambulance, and she says the ambulance driver was instructed to take her to the nearest facility."

Sierra explained the reason as we made our way back to the rest of the family.

"Alex, they said they had to take her there."

My mom stepped forward and tried to calm me down.

"Unbelievable," I said. "Let's just go. I need to see what the hell is going on."

We reached the hospital in record time. As soon as I entered Granny's room, I knew the damage had already been done. She was in a completely vegetative state. I knelt beside her bed and prayed. Fighting back my tears, I proceeded to the nurses' station and demanded to see the Director of Nurses and the physician taking care of my grandmother.

While I awaited their arrival, my mom pulled me to the side.

"Alex, she's not gonna get better, is she?"

"No, momma, she's not."

"But Alex, she talked to us yesterday and the doctor planned to discharge her in a few days. What happened?"

From the looks of it, she was on the verge of breaking down and I wasn't ready to deal with that just yet.

"I don't know, but believe me, we will have some answers before we leave here today."

"What seems to be the problem?"

The Director of Nurses' asked as she made her way to the nurses' station. She was noticeably irritated by the summons and made no attempt to hide it.

"Good morning to you, too," I said. "And you are….?"

Under ordinary circumstances, I would have called her out on the nasty little attitude, but I decided to let her make it.

"I'm the Director of Nurses, and I was told you wanted to speak with me."

"I'm Attorney Alexandra Phillips and this is my family," I said and offered a handshake.

Lead by example. My military training served me well. The DON severely lacked manners, but I refused to stoop to her level. After my introduction, the immediate change in her attitude was apparent to everyone at the nurses' station. Most likely, she came prepared to offer my family a litany of generic excuses as to the reason for the sudden change in my grandmother's condition. Hopefully, she was intelligent enough to know that she was not dealing with the typical uneducated, easily appeased family member.

"Ms. Phillips, how can I assist you?"

Much better, I thought and proceeded.

"I need you to obtain a complete copy of my grandmother's records. Today. I also requested your staff to contact my grandmother's physician, but since he's failed to respond, I need you to arrange for a meeting. I will be here promptly at nine tomorrow morning, and I expect him to be here as well."

The look she gave me was one that I was accustomed to. It was that unmistakable look of surprise from a White person unaccustomed to taking directives from an African-American woman.

"Are we clear Nurse Stevens?" I asked, getting her name from the name badge since she failed to properly introduce herself.

"I'll see what I can do, Attorney Phillips, but I can't guarantee ...."

Not interested in excuses, I stopped her in midsentence.

"Nurse Stevens, according to your patients' rights policy, the doctor is duty bound to communicate with the patient or the patient's family. If you or the physician is unwilling to follow your own policy, there are repercussions. Again, I will be here at nine in the morning. Sharp. Thanks for your time."

I dismissed her and returned to my grandmother's room.

It was hard to see her like this. By now, the seriousness of the situation was clear to my mom and her sisters, and they began to fall apart. I needed to clear my head. As I made my way towards the door, I was met by an employee from medical records. She held a copy of Granny's records.

"Attorney Phillips?"

"Yes, I'm Attorney Phillips."

"Your grandmother's records," she said with a smile and handed over the file.

"Contact me directly if you need anything else," she said.

She handed me a card and left the room. A potential ally, I thought, just in case.

"Can you guys ride with me?"

I turned and asked Sierra and Lenny who stood quietly in the corner.

"I need to get these records sent to my office in DC, and I need to get over to the police station to talk to Yasmin."

"Sure, Alex, I'll go with you."

Lenny jumped at the chance to get out of the hospital room. By now, he was overwhelmed with being the only male in the mist of four grieving women.

"You guys go ahead. I'm gonna stay here."

Sierra was really shaken by Granny's condition. So was I, but I had to keep it together. I figured the hospital couldn't do any more damage than they'd already done, especially with everyone there.

Thankfully, I remembered the directions to my friend's law office. The records were scanned and forwarded to my office within minutes. I'd already instructed my paralegal to drop what she was doing.

"Karen, I need you to go through that record with a fine tooth comb, and I need the findings like yesterday. It's my grandmother."

"Alex, I'm so sorry. I'm on it. Give me a couple of hours, and I'll have something for you. How are you holding up?"

"Not good, Karen. I'm looking at the records as we speak, but I can't...."

I couldn't finish the sentence. Lenny took the phone and finished the conversation for me. Then, he put his arm around me in comfort.

"It's gonna be ok, Alex. Go ahead and get it all out. You have a lot of work to do and your family is depending on you."

Thankfully, my family wasn't there. I didn't want them to see me like this. For the second time in two days, I was crying in this stranger's arms. The thought of this made me cry even harder. Why didn't I have someone of my own to comfort me? Not only was I losing my grandmother, I still had to figure out what was going on with Yasmin. Was the nightmare ever going to end? As Lenny and I made our way to the county jail, I got a call from Latrice.

"Alex, have you spoken with Yasmin?"

"No, I'm headed there right now. What's up?"

"Yori talked to Arlissa. Keith was up to no good just as we suspected."

According to Latrice's second-hand account, Keith was probably grooming Arlissa, a common tactic used by abusers to gain the child's trust. Thinking back to my survivor's class, Arlissa was an excellent target. In reality, no child was really safe around Keith, however, Arlissa was a soft target. Clearly suffering from emotional neglect and lack of self-confidence, Arlissa soaked up attention like a sponge. On the surface, I suppose Yasmin was responsible for making Arlissa a soft target due to her less than appealing lifestyle and bad habits. However, there was so much more to it than that. Keith was, without a doubt, both the cause and effect for every aspect of the day's events, to include his own death.

164

"Wow. What a sick bastard. I hate to say it, but the world is definitely better off without him. Listen, I'm almost there. I'll hit you up as soon as I'm done."

After completing all of the red tape requirements for attorney/council visits, it was very obvious, Yasmin was on the verge of a breakdown. After speaking with her, the first order of business was to request a bail hearing and get her the hell out of there ASAP. Getting the hearing was an easy enough task, but I wasn't sure if the judge in that particular jurisdiction would actually grant bail for a murder case and if so, how much? The Eighth Amendment prohibits excessive bail. However, severity and nature of the crime were determining factors, along with flight potential. From what I heard, Judge Bufford was pretty tough, but we got our answer the next morning. Bail was set at seventy-five thousand dollars. Yasmin was able to give me the name of a bondsman, who actually attended high school with me. I opted to just pay the ten percent bond instead of waiting for Yasmin's mom to scrape it together. That process would have taken days. She was immediately released after the mandatory ten percent posted. Now that Yasmin was situated at home with her mother and her daughter, I could focus my attention on Granny.

After reading Karen's report, I was ready for my nine o'clock meeting with the hospital staff. I got there early enough to see Granny before the meeting and found her condition pretty much the same. She was completely unresponsive. With tears in my eyes, I left her room and headed over to the administrative suite. Someone had some explaining to do.

Not only was my grandmother's physician present for the meeting, the hospital attorney was there as well.

"Good morning. I'm attorney Alexandra Phillips and I'm here for a 9:00 meeting," I informed the receptionist.

"Good morning, Ms. Phillips, right this way," the administrative assistant said and led me into the next room.

"Good morning Attorney Phillips."

The Director of Nurses greeted me and extended her hand for a handshake. Apparently, someone had gotten some manners in the twenty-four hour period since our last encounter.

"This is Dr. Shah. He's been taking care of your grandmother since her admission."

"Attorney Phillips," he nodded without bothering to stand or extend his hand.

Cool. So, I was dealing with yet another arrogant physician. This was how I earned a living, and I did it well. However, this time, it was personal, and I was going from zero to a hundred real fast.

"And this is Attorney Webb, our hospital attorney."

Attorney Webb stood and shook my hand before she returned to her seat. I came straight to the point.

"Look, I don't have a lot of time to go over all of my concerns, as they are many," I announced and proceeded to distribute the twenty-page list of violations.

"Attorney Phillips, I understand your concern for your grandmother, but keep in mind, she is up in age."

Dr. Shah spoke while he squirmed uncomfortably in his chair.

"Your grandmother suffered severe brain damage due to ongoing seizure activity, as I am sure you are aware. We have implemented several medication regimens, but unfortunately, she has not responded very well."

"Dr. Shah, if you would turn to page seven of the document. Irreversible brain damage is at the top of my list of concerns. From all indications, your failure to adequately control the seizure activity in a timely manner or implement measures to protect her brain is the direct cause of the irreversible brain damage. Her age had little to do with it."

"Attorney Phillips…."

"Excuse me, Dr. Shah, but I was not finished speaking," I said with enough authority for everyone in the room to recognize I meant business.

"According to the standard of care for patients admitted for persistent or poorly controlled seizures, the patient is to be transferred to the intensive care unit and sedated in order to circumvent damage to the brain. According to hospital records, my grandmother has yet to see the inside of your intensive care unit."

"If you would continue reading on page seven, you will find an entry regarding the improper use of an intravenous catheter on the day of her admission. Clearly, it is impossible to deliver intravenous medication without appropriate intravenous access."

I paused, then continued with my attention directed to the Director of Nurse.

"According to the nursing records, the intravenous catheter was dysfunctional for approximately twenty-four hours, during which time my grandmother failed to receive the anti-seizure medication. This is quite unacceptable, and I strongly recommend the implementation of a performance improvement plan to address the sub-standard nursing care".

"On day number two of her admission, my grandmother received a regular meal, per Dr. Shah's written order. Correct me if I'm wrong, but according to the standard of care for patients diagnosed with active seizures, the patient is to receive nothing by mouth until the seizures are controlled. Is this true, Dr. Shah?"

"You are correct."

"Would you or someone from the nursing staff care to explain how or why my grandmother was given a steak dinner when her seizures were not yet controlled?"

"There must be some mistake. I wouldn't have written such an order..."

"Is this not your signature?"

I walked over to his seat and presented a copy of the written order.

"Is it your signature, Dr. Shah?"

"It appears so."

"According to the x-rays taken upon admission, her lungs were clear and there were no signs of pneumonia. Please turn to page eight of your binders. A chest X-ray obtained the day after she was given the steak dinner is indicative of pneumonia. Would anyone care to explain to me the mechanism of action of aspiration pneumonia?"

No one said a word.

What happened to my grandmother was very clear and it didn't take a rocket scientist to figure it out. As a result of poor nursing care, she received none of the anti-seizure medication for the first twenty-four hours and was then provided a steak meal, which was probably aspirated into her lungs as a result of the ongoing seizures. The end result was aspiration pneumonia and inadequate oxygen levels in her brain.

"Uh, well...." Dr. Shah stuttered.

"If you can't answer the question, Dr. Shah, perhaps your attorney could assist you," I stated as the anger made its way to the surface.

"Attorney Phillips, on behalf of the hospital, you have my deepest sympathy and apology."

The hospital attorney finally spoke in the face of my fury.

"I did a little chart review of my own in preparation for this meeting and was disturbed at the findings. Several quality of care issues have been identified, and they will be addressed. Further investigation into this matter is underway as we speak and I can assure you, every effort will be made to address your concerns," she continued while shooting mini daggers at Dr. Shah.

"Due to the seriousness of your grandmother's condition and in light of the numerous violations in the standard of care, I am inclined to offer you and your family a settlement for damages."

I was completely floored by her last statement. An offer for settlement this soon was unprecedented. Apparently, the attorney was smart enough to grasp the enormity of errors involved in the management of my grandmother's illness and was willing to cut their losses sooner than later.

"Interesting. In all of my years of practice, this is a first. I appreciate the gesture, but my family is not in a position to accept an offer at this time. As I stated earlier, the damage to her brain is irreversible. We could lose her today or she could remain in the vegetative state for the next five to ten years," I replied and willed myself not to cry as I spoke.

"On page twelve of your binders, you will find an official letter of complaint addressed to the Louisiana Board of Medicine detailing the breaches in the standard of care. The letter clearly identifies Dr. Shah as my grandmother's primary physician," I said while looking directly at the charlatan responsible for this mess.

I could see the anger and irritation in his face, but I didn't care. According to Karen, this physician had been sued more than five times in the last two years for medical malpractice resulting in death. While I'd never been one to deliberately go after anyone's livelihood, I was going to make certain he never practiced in this country again.

"The accrediting body for the hospital has been apprised of the poor nursing quality and overall unsafe environment."

I turned to the Director of Nurses, who squirmed in her seat as well.

"Nurses are the lifeline between the patient and the physician. Your nurses failed miserably."

"Just to be clear, monetary compensation in any amount will never rectify the pain and suffering you have caused my family. My primary goal is to prevent this from happening to another family. Thanks for your time."

I gathered my things and headed to the door. I didn't bother to look back. By now, I was in tears and eager to get back to my grandmother's room. Getting her transferred out of this death trap was next on my list of things to do that morning.

"Alex, she's gone!"

Sierra wailed and nearly knocked me over when I exited the elevator across the hall from Granny's room.

"What do you mean she's gone? Are they running more tests?"

I loosened her grip and reached for the door.

"No, Alex. She's gone. She just slipped away....."

Sierra's words finally hit me when I heard the grief in the room.

"NOOOOO!!!!!!!"

I screamed and fell to my knees beside the hospital bed.

Chapter Nineteen

Alex

"To everything, there is a season and a time to every purpose under the heaven, a time to be born, and a time to die, a time to plant and a time to pluck up that which is planted, a time to kill and a time to heal, a time to break down and a time to build up..." (Ecclesiastes 3:1-3).

I woke up at my parent's house to find Lawrence sitting on the bed next to me. From what I could gather, my sister had called him the day before to let him know what was going on and to ask him to come down. He arrived shortly before Granny passed away. At some point, I was given a tranquilizer, and Lawrence was forced to take over. My family was a wreck. He arranged for her body to be taken to Peaceful Valley Funeral home and he took care of all of the business concerning the funeral.

The funeral was held at Granny's church the following Saturday. The tears flowed freely and the sounds of agonizing misery were audible throughout the service. Although it was a time honored custom in our neck of the woods, I never understood the "Obituary Silently Read" section of the funeral programs. No one ever waited to read the obituary. It was the first thing a person did if they were lucky enough to obtain a funeral program. By the time we reached that segment of the program, I'd already read Granny's obituary three times. After reading her date of birth and date of departure over and over again, I did the math and discovered something that hadn't occurred to me until that very moment. If my oldest aunt was seventy-three, and my grandmother was eighty-six, Granny must have been thirteen when she gave birth to her first child.

Thirteen. I guess this sort of answered all of my questions. As a child, I remembered thinking Aunt Flora seemed more like Granny's sister than her daughter. To add to the confusion, Aunt Flora was raised by my great-grandmother. Granny eventually married my grandfather, who was clearly not Aunt Flora's father, and they started a family. Talk about confusing.

My tears were now a result of not only the tragic loss of my grandmother, but also for the little girl who was forced into womanhood at such a young age. I could only imagine how it all happened. Some sick bastard had obviously taken advantage of her. Perhaps this was the reason for Granny's indifference to Sierra's confession so many years ago. Yet, another secret revealed. There had to be a name for this seemingly perpetual cycle of abuse. So far, I was able to identify no less than four generations of abuse, starting with Granny and ending with Yasmin and Yori. If Yasmin hadn't put an end to it, Arlissa would have been the fifth generation.

In traditional Louisiana fashion, my grandmother was crowned with an ornate rhinestone tiara as the soloist sang an old southern gospel song originally performed by Thomas Whitfield, "I shall wear a crown…" The solemn arrangement of the song coupled with the theatrical lifting of the casket into the air as it is slowly carried out of the church never failed to elicit, or in my family's case, augment the uncontrollable display of sorrow and grief.

The loss of the foundational component of a family with issues such as ours was a huge blow. In the days leading up to the funeral, the family was lost. Everyone functioned instinctively, with seemingly very little purpose or hope. The loss was sure to result in further dysfunction, or so I thought. To my surprise, picking up the pieces was far less chaotic than I predicted. The biggest concern was for Sierra and her children. Their lives and their mother's life were totally dependent on

Granny. Sierra was finally forced to step up to the plate and become a mother. Surprisingly, she seemed to embrace her responsibility.

Lenny, who finally came to terms with Tiffany's death, remained at Sierra's side throughout the transition and scored major points with the family. After tying up loose ends with his "real estate business" in Vegas, he returned with an engagement ring and the keys to a brand new house for Sierra and the kids. With money he'd earned in Vegas, he purchased the seafood restaurant on the boardwalk, "Sistah's." The restaurant was known for its authentic Louisiana cuisine and uplifting southern ambiance, but to everyone's surprise, it was going belly up. Thanks to Lenny's acumen as a businessman, the restaurant thrived again in no time and plans were made to open a second restaurant on the opposite side of town. Sierra chipped in from time to time on the management side of the operation, however, her primary focus was her kids. She was determined to make up for lost time.

Latrice and J.T. moved into Granny's old house. Since I was the official owner of the house, we made a deal. She could stay rent-free as long as she respected the premises: no strange visitors, drug dealers, etc. If she failed to hold up her end of the bargain, she would be evicted immediately, no questions asked.

With just a few months to prepare for Yasmin's trial, I returned to DC with a heavy heart. In order to save Yasmin, I would have to unveil more than two decades of family secrets. Keith's sisters and his wife had already made their positions clear. They didn't appreciate the ill-talk about the dead since he was not here to defend himself. According to them, no amount of proof would justify Yasmin's actions. I finally gave up. They could hear the gory details directly from me or wait to hear it at the trial with everyone else.

After Granny's death, Lawrence became the only constant source of optimism for me. By now, he was fully aware of the hidden dynamics of my family. While he was not enthusiastic about my decision to represent Yasmin, he understood my sense of obligation and the guilt. He spent every other weekend in DC, and I traveled to Florida whenever my schedule permitted. After years of confusion and lost time, it seemed we were finally headed in the right direction.

Chapter Twenty

I decided to go home a few weeks before the trial in order to prepare my witnesses. Crime of passion would be Yasmin's primary defense. The basis for this defense is to prove the defendant acted immediately upon the rise of passion, without time for premeditation. The overall goal of this defense is to eliminate the charge by proving the action was justified. Under the right circumstances, it was not uncommon for compassionate juries to acquit impassioned defendants. In lieu of an acquittal, a reduction of the homicide charge to manslaughter and avoiding the death penalty is the alternative goal. If this particular crime had taken place in Texas instead of Louisiana, Yasmin would have little to worry about. In law school, the crime of passion defense was referred to as the *Law of Texas*, since Texas jurors are consistently lenient toward impassioned defendants.

While I was confident about the defense strategy, all three of my star witnesses were hampered with checkered pasts. I fully expected the prosecutor to use this information to discredit their testimony, however, I was prepared to use the negative information to my advantage. In order to do so, I would have to prove their negative pasts were directly related to the abuse they suffered at the hands of Keith.

Sierra and Yasmin could probably hold their own on the witness stand. Latrice was going to be the wild card for several reasons. First of all, the twenty years of drug abuse had wreaked havoc on her physical appearance. As a result, operation transformation was at the top of my list. Thankfully, she agreed to a full mouth extraction and a new set of dentures. With the new set of dentures, half of the mission was complete. Next, I made an appointment with a local Mary Kay representative who happened to be a friend of Camilla's. After about four hours of intense therapy, which involved several rounds of cleanser, exfoliator and moisturizer, Latrice's face began to take on a softer appearance. This was followed by make-up application and re-application until the right color combination was achieved. Day number three was a trip to a private downtown boutique. Worst case scenario, the trial could possibly last up to ten days. The goal was to select up to five professional-looking outfits that were interchangeable or easily accessorized for a different look. Day number four was a trip to the hair salon. This one would take a while. Latrice was mainly interested in a long sew-in, the longer the better, according to her, with a trendy burgundy rinse. After going back and forth over the color and the length, she finally threatened to go out and purchase one of those dreadful lace front wigs. By this point, I was losing my patience. Finally, the stylist stepped in with a recommendation that we could both live with---an asymmetrical, shoulder length sew-in. The color we chose was jet black with light brown highlights better known as FS1-B37.

According to Latrice, she hadn't used any hard drugs in over a month, but she still used marijuana on a daily basis.

"Alex, you can't expect me to give up everything just like that," she said with a finger snap, "it's the only way I'm gonna be able to get on that witness stand."

"Latrice, I need you to promise me, weed only. Nothing else."

"I'm good, Alex. I got this."

"Ok. I'm picking you up tomorrow around noon. You, Sierra, and Yasmin are going to experience a mock trial. My law school buddy will act as the prosecutor, and I will be the defense attorney. Be ready by noon," I said and pulled out of Granny's driveway. "And wear something nice."

"I'm ready, Alex. This is long overdue."

"Yes, it is. See you tomorrow, Latrice."

The intricacies of Louisiana law were intimidating, to say the least. In addition to the distinction of having the lengthiest and most challenging bar exam in the United States, it is also the only Napoleonic legal system ("civil law") in the country. "Common law" is the legal system for the remaining forty-nine states. As a result, the overlapping and conflicting statutes within the Louisiana Criminal Code are often difficult to grasp in the appropriate context, even for the most seasoned criminal attorney. For example, premeditation or planning is required for a first-degree murder charge in most states. In Louisiana, specific intent is the only requirement for first-degree murder. In addition, death by lethal injection or natural life are the only possible sentences for first degree murder in the state of Louisiana.

From what I could remember from school, it was not uncommon for family members of the victim to petition prosecutors for the removal of the death penalty option for first degree murder convictions. The petitions were made for various reasons, but typically occurred in cases involving close family members. It was a long shot, but in light of the undeniable pattern of abuse over the course of no less than twenty years, I made an appeal to Keith's wife and sisters for a petition to the prosecution to remove the death penalty option. Such would not be the case, thanks to the wife and one of the sisters. The wife's unwillingness to remove the death penalty option was understandable, but I was a little surprised and offended by his sister's attitude. Surely she could see that her brother's behavior was the mediating factor which lead to his death. When everything was said and done, Yasmin would be facing life in prison or lethal injection if the crime of passion defense failed.

As a matter of historical fact, ambitious prosecutors tend to aim for the highest murder charge, even when the evidence is insufficient. During opening statements, the prosecutor wasted no time expressing his desire for "nothing less than a conviction of murder in the first degree and lethal injection". According to him, the *ready availability of the murder weapon* was evidence of specific intent. While this was a plausible theory, it was one that I was completely ready to defend. Since Louisiana happened to be an "open carry" state, the "ready availability" of the weapon would be easy to explain. Furthermore, I thought it would be extremely hard to find a juror in Louisiana who at a minimum did not own a gun or were not staunch supporters of the Second Amendment Right to bear arms.

The prosecution's case was presented as expected: numerous character witnesses to sing Keith's praises and a few eye-witnesses to confirm and re-confirm, "He was just standing there minding his business..." Standing there minding his business, my ass. While I tried to avoid placing Arlissa on the witness stand, if push came to shove, she was prepared to disclose Keith's exact comments to her that day.

Yasmin became more and more anxious with each passing witness. I tried to reassure her.

"Yasmin, take a deep breath. We're doing fine. You cannot allow the jury to see any sign of negativity. They are watching your every move."

On the surface, the prosecution seemed to have an air-tight case. But at this point, not one piece of compelling evidence for "specific intent" had been presented by the prosecution. Overall, the evidence was mediocre at best. After only a day and a half of testimony, the prosecution rested. However, the actual strength of the prosecution's case would depend on the prosecutor's ability to systematically discredit the testimony of our star witnesses. I refused to think about that. We would cross that bridge when we got there.

I was ready for the cross-examination the next day, beginning with Yasmin and Yori's neighbor from down the street. She was a well-respected citizen in the small community, and the principal at the local high school. In her testimony as a character witness for the decedent, she sang Keith's praises along with everyone else. However, there were a few things missing from her direct testimony. I planned to jar her memory during the cross examination.

"Mrs. Johnson, can you state for the record again, your occupation?"

"I'm the principal at Southbend high school."

"How long have you held that position?"

"For 23 years."

"Earlier in your testimony, you mentioned you were the principal at the school when the decedent attended. Were you the principal at the time of the defendant's attendance?"

"Yes, I was."

"What type of student was the defendant?"

"Well, she seemed to be more interested in boys than anything else, and that's putting it nicely."

"Other than being boy-crazy, is there anything else you care to tell me about the defendant?"

"No, not anything specific."

"Your honor, may I submit Exhibit "A" to the witness?"

"You may."

"Mrs. Johnson, can you describe the document for the jury and read the first few lines please?"

"It's an incident report dated October 8, 1989. Student presented to office this morning in an emotional, disheveled state. Unable to determine exact cause of student's behavior. Parents notified, later dismissed into the custody of mother at 10:30 am."

"Do you recall this event?"

"As a matter of fact, I do."

"In the report, you stated you were unable to determine the exact cause of the student's behavior. Did the student offer any type of explanation?"

"Yes, she did."

"Do you recall the explanation?"

"Vaguely."

"What was her explanation?"

"I can't remember her exact words, but she basically said she was tired of her cousin, Keith. She said that he was sexually abusing her," the principal stated reluctantly.

"What was your response?"

"I told her to stop lying."

"May I ask your reason for discounting her claim?"

"Keith was not like that. And besides, Yasmin was in the "fast girl" crowd. I just assumed she was lying."

"Really? If I'm not mistaken, you're obligated to report such claims, whether you believe them to be true or not, yet you opted to overlook the defendant's claim. Am I correct?"

"Yes. You are correct, but I..."

"No further questions for this witness, your honor."

This incident had been far removed from Yasmin's memory. However, my persistence for disclosure of even the smallest detail and the long hours spent recounting specific events with Yasmin and Yori paid off.

The final witness for cross-examination was Keith's older sister, Rebecca.

"Can you describe for the court, your relationship with your brother, as children?"

"It was like any other sister-brother relationship, I suppose."

She was not going to make this easy, so I decided to get straight to the point.

"Mrs. Abrams, how old was your brother when he was kicked out of your home?"

"Objection, your honor," the prosecutor shouted.

"Over ruled. Answer the question please."

"If you're referring to the point at which he stopped living with us, he was around thirteen."

Keith's sister answered me in a calm voice, however, her facial expression told a different story.

"Can you recall any particular reason or incident that may have occurred immediately prior to Keith moving out of your home? Please remember you're under oath".

"My dad asked him to leave....for exposing himself to Carolyn," she stated hesitantly.

"Carolyn is your younger sister, correct?"

"Yes?"

"How old was she at the time of this incident?"

"Four."

"Can you speak a little louder, Mrs. Abrams? How old was your sister when the event occurred?"

"Four-years-old!"

She practically shouted before she clenched her mouth shut.

"No further questions your honor."

Wow, another score for the defense, I thought as I returned to my seat. This little piece of information was provided to me by my grandmother's sister just two days before the trial began. I always assumed there was a specific reason for Keith's nomadic life. Now, I knew for sure. Yet another secret revealed. I presented my witnesses without a hitch. I was very pleased with Yasmin and Latrice's testimony, but I was completely exhausted when we finally finished.

"The court is adjourned for the day. We will resume tomorrow at eight."

The judge must have read my mind. Enough was enough.

Chapter Twenty-One

As suspected, the prosecutor saved his ammunition for my key witnesses. While I was pleased with their testimonies and the manner in which they conveyed their experiences, the cross examination was a nightmare. By the time he was finished highlighting the drug abuse, prostitution, and child abandonment allegations, the chance of a sympathetic appeal from the jury was out of the question.

One of our strongest pieces of evidence was Latrice and Sierra's testimony regarding Keith's confession. The part of the confession pertaining to Mr. Peabody was particularly important because it established the principal of cause and effect. Juries are more receptive to this type of evidence. For example, Keith was a victim of sexual abuse, therefore, he became an abuser. Because Yasmin was abused by Keith, she snapped when she saw him talking to her daughter. Plain and simple.

Since the majority of the "confession" testimony was declared hearsay and not allowed into evidence, a different strategy was required in order to introduce the evidence in its entirety. The first order of business was the "introduction" of Mr. Peabody by a credible witness. Granny's sister, Aunt Thelma, was just the person for the job since she was the only living person with first-hand knowledge about him.

After Aunt Thelma's testimony, Sierra or Latrice would be called for redirect. Once again, the confession testimony would be met with objection due to hearsay, however, this time I had a strong argument for an exception to hearsay. In a last ditch effort to regain some lost ground, I mentally tossed a coin and chose Latrice for redirect.

"Your honor, may I approach?"

"Your honor, I would like to call a new witness to the stand, Mrs. Thelma Harris. In light of the direction the trial has taken, I believe she may be able to provide vital evidence to the defense of my client...."

"Your honor, I'm pretty sure Attorney Phillips is accustomed to all types of legal shenanigans up in DC, but down here, we like to follow the rules. You rested your case," the prosecutor's rhetorical interruption put me on edge.

"With all due respect, the legal system in DC is nothing compared to what I've seen down here. Don't forget, I'm a native Louisianan. Your honor, I'm fighting for my client's life, and in light of the abuse she's already suffered at the hands of the deceased, I believe she has a right to present any and all potentially redeeming evidence."

"Attorney Phillips, I will allow the testimony only if it is specific to your defense."

"I believe it is, your honor."

"You may proceed. Mrs. Harris, please come forward."

Having a female judge was definitely favorable under the circumstances, I thought as Aunt Thelma was sworn in. She understood.

"Mrs. Harris, can you state your relationship to the deceased please?"

"Well, I suppose you could say Keith was related to me by marriage. Keith's grandfather, Peabody, was my sister's cousin-in-law."

"So, to simplify the relationship for the record, your brother-in-law was Mr. Peabody's cousin. Is that correct?"

"I suppose that's a good way to say it. We all lived so close together that we just considered everybody family. After a while, you forget just how it came to be."

"As a child, Keith lived with Mr. Peabody periodically, is that correct?"

"Objection, where is this going?" asked the prosecutor.

"Your honor, this line of questioning is pertinent to the defense."

"Go on, but you're treading thin, Attorney Phillips."

"Yes, your honor. Mrs. Harris, can you tell us anything about Mr. Peabody that would be relevant to this case?"

I couldn't make it any plainer than that, I thought.

"Well, the only thing I can say about Peabody, rest his soul, is he had his funny ways. We all grew up together, and he was what we used to call fresh, if you know what I mean."

"Mrs. Harris, can you explain for the jury, the term "fresh"?"

"Well, what I mean is…well, uh…it didn't matter who or what, young or old, boy or girl, he was just fresh with everybody. In a sexual way is what I mean. You understand?"

"Thank you Mrs. Harris. No further questions. Your witness," I said to the prosecutor.

"I see no reason to question this witness", he arrogantly declined.

"In that case, I'd like to call Latrice Taylor back to the stand for re-direct, your honor."

I had butterflies in my stomach while I waited for the deputy to retrieve Latrice from the witness room. This was it. The kitchen sink and all.

"Mrs. Taylor, referring back to the incident occurring on December 27th of last year, was there ever any mention of Mr. Peabody?"

"Objection your honor. Hearsay."

"Your honor, if I may? The testimony being presented speaks directly to the cause of my client's actions. Mrs. Harris' testimony, as anecdotal as it seems, provides substantially creditable evidence, which speaks to the potential cause of the behavior and the mind-set of the decedent, which eventually lead to the actions of my client. Since neither Mr. Peabody nor the decedent are available for testimony, for obvious reasons, an exception to hearsay is applicable", I responded, using a little rhetoric of my own.

"Objection over ruled," the judge stated after a moment of consideration.

"This better be good, Attorney Phillips. Answer the question," she said to Latrice.

"Was there ever any mention of Mr. Peabody during the decedent's confession?"

"Yes, there was."

"Can you tell the court what was said Ms. Taylor?"

"Objection!"

"Restate the question," instructed the judge.

"During the conversation in question, did the decedent make any comments concerning Mr. Peabody?"

"He said Mr. Peabody was the reason that he did the things he did."

The courtroom erupted with outrage from Keith's supporters.

"Hearsay!" screamed the prosecutor

"Order in the court!"

The judge banged her gavel and demanded silence.

"I have it on tape," Latrice said loudly over the noise.

Suddenly, the room went completely silent.

"Your honor, may I approach?"

Chapter Twenty-two

Court was immediately adjourned as Keith's family erupted in dismay over Latrice's testimony. I was just as shocked as everyone else because Latrice had never mentioned anything about a tape to me. At the request of the prosecutor, the tape was given to a forensic voice analyst for authentication. I was a little skeptical about the potential outcome, but to my surprise, it was Keith's voice. But how?

According to Latrice, she recorded the entire conversation and put it away for safe keeping with the thought that it would come in handy if we ever decided to take action against Keith. Apparently the tape was misplaced shortly thereafter. Perhaps it was divine intervention or simply the newfound mental clarity that Latrice experienced as a result of her "sobriety" (weed only) that led her to the tape. Miraculously, she found it at Granny's house in the same place that she left it.

"Things weren't looking good for Yasmin. So, when you told me I was going back on the witness stand, I knew I had to find that tape. J.T. and I turned that house upside down looking for it last night. J.T. found it. It was under Granny's mattress," Latrice explained when we departed the courthouse for the day.

Closing arguments began the following day. As suspected, the prosecutor continued his attempts to discredit all of the witnesses for the defense, and he reminded the jurors of the "readily availability" of the murder weapon which, according to him, was indisputable evidence of intent.

Then, it was my turn. Yasmin was in good shape with the jury. The tape alone was enough evidence to assure an acquittal. Therefore, I used my closing argument as an opportunity to purge. I wanted the jury and the family to know in no uncertain terms, that Keith was a depraved sociopath:

"Ladies and gentlemen of the jury, as a defense attorney, it is never my intention to place a victim on trial. However, we have to be clear about the real victims in this case. The depraved indifference of the decedent, Mr. Keith Baynes, is irrefutable and the evidence presented to you by the defense is a classic example of murder actuated in "the heat of passion" or as a "crime of passion". Over the course of no less than two decades, Mr. Baynes not only robbed his victims of a normal childhood, he systematically destroyed their lives. You heard the testimony of two of Mr. Bayne's victims in graphic detail. The prosecution has gone through great lengths to discredit the character and testimony of these witnesses by highlighting the mistakes and bad choices that they've made over the years. In reality, he provided support for the 'cause and effect' theory which is associated with this type of abuse. According to the psychologist's testimony, the bad choices and mistakes that the prosecution so eloquently identified, were directly related to the abuse they suffered at the hands of the decedent which began when they were just four and five years old. I have to ask. How would you feel, Mr. Prosecutor, if these horrible things happened to your daughter?

According to the expert testimony of the child psychologist, the long term effects of sexual abuse in children include depression, guilt, shame, denial, anxiety, self-blame, low self-esteem, drug abuse, sexual dysfunction, bonding issues, post-traumatic stress, and the list goes on and on. In light of this testimony, can you blame the victims for the bad choices they made? Because of the abuse that these ladies suffered, they never had a chance for a normal childhood or anything else for that matter. Because of Mr. Baynes' position and influence in the family and his ability to instill fear and shame within each of his victims, they literally suffered in silence as they carried this horrible secret. As a result, they developed unhealthy coping mechanisms for day to day survival. It had to end.

On the day in question, the defendant snapped. Plain and simple. And while her actions may have been intentional, they were not premeditated. The very sight of Mr. Baynes in a conversation with her daughter caused the defendant to take immediate action for one purpose and one purpose only...she had to put an end to this vicious cycle of abuse once and for all. Ask yourselves this question, what would you have done? If your answer to that question lines up in any way with the actions of the defendant, you have to find her not guilty. This was a crime of passion. Nothing more, nothing less."

Yasmin was acquitted of all charges.

The truth had finally come out once and for all, and the manner in which it emerged was priceless, thanks to Latrice. Keith effectively conveyed the secret that we carried with us from childhood in his own voice, using his own words. While his sisters finally accepted things for what they were, his wife was still in denial about the depravity of her deceased husband. Like many child molesters, Keith was charming and loving, and appeared to display none predatory traits. Honestly, if I didn't have first-hand experience, I might have doubted the claims against Keith as well. Sadly, Keith's son would grow up to learn of his father's shame just as the descendants of Mr. Peabody had learn of his. Perhaps now, the healing could began.

Epilogue

Just a year ago, I was grieving the loss of my grandmother and defending my cousin in a capital murder case. Today, I was nursing my son. A few days after the trial, I took a long overdue trip to my doctor back in DC. The fatigue was finally getting the best of me. She took one look at me and ordered a pregnancy test. It was positive.

Everything should have fallen into place after that, but it didn't. Lawrence and I weren't headed down the aisle any time soon. I had no answers for my family regarding our strange relationship and thankfully, they stopped asking. I was resigned to the possibility that I would be raising my son alone. I still had a lot of soul searching to do regarding the way things turned out with me and Lawrence. Was I too emotionally damaged to maintain a healthy relationship? Was Demetrius correct in his assessment of my relationship with Lawrence? He was convinced that Lawrence had commitment issues. It would definitely explain Lawrence's contentment with long distance relationships. In all fairness, I couldn't leave out the issue of forgiveness; and therefore, I had to acknowledge my role in the demise of the relationship. Had he really forgiven me for my indiscretion with Demetrius? He said he had, but I was not convinced.

My family was finally coming to terms to life without Granny. Lenny and Sierra's relationship seemed to be thriving. At some point after they were married, Sierra finally told him about the hysterectomy. To her surprise, he already knew.

"But you never said anything", Sierra was astonished and relieved. "When did you find out?"

"I made it my business to know everything there was to know about each of you. You should know that. To answer your question, I reviewed your medical records before we ever met."

"But how? Medical records are confidential". Maybe he was covering for Janell.

"I had my ways", he said smugly.

They are now in the final stages of adopting a beautiful baby girl from Haiti. For once, Sierra was truly happy. But her past was ever present in her mind. She shuddered at the thought of some of the things she did before Lenny rescued her. He had to be the most understanding man on the face of the earth. How else could he love her so completely? Sierra eventually garnered enough courage to ask him if his love for her had anything to do with her uncanny resemblance to Tiffany. The notion was quickly expelled.

"I love you for you, Sierra... in spite of your flaws. I never told you this, but allowing you to work for me was the hardest thing I ever had to do. I tried to convince myself that lust was the reason for my immediate attraction to you. However, lust is a transient, fleeting emotion, based primarily on physical attraction and initial perceptions. Love is an enduring emotion. It allows you to see beyond imperfections. When I met you, your beauty was covered by bruises and scars and you were in profession that required you to share your body with countless other men. Somehow, I was able to see beyond all of that. I think I fell in love with you the moment I walked into your hospital room. I fought it for as long as I could, but in the end I had to follow my heart."

She couldn't ask for a better answer. He nailed it. I was relieved to be out of the business and away from the Vegas scene, but my biggest regret was leaving my friends behind-- especially Janell and Cindy. We had so many things in common and I think it was the reason we hit it off so well.

"Lenny, I'm happier than I've ever been in my life, but I'm feeling a little guilty about leaving Janell and Cindy behind".

"I figured you would. Just to let you know, I offered all of the girls an opportunity to move on. They turned me down."

"What kind of opportunity did you have in mind?"

"I was thinking along the lines of a severance package so to speak--money to relocate and maybe enough to go back to school and take up a trade".

"And they turned you down?"

Who in their right mind would turn down an opportunity like that? After thinking about it, I sort of understood. It was the only life they knew; and for them, the prospect of trying something new was not a viable option. The years of mental and physical abuse had completely destroyed their ability to aspire or envision anything better than the life they already had. I was proud of Lenny for trying and my love for him escalated even more. What did I do to deserve a man like him...?

To everyone's surprise, Latrice was finally free of her addiction. She was working full time and concentrating her efforts on keeping her son from making the same mistakes she made. She had her hands full, but at least she was trying. While she never really had any confidence in psychologists or substance abuse counseling, she was now a believer. She and JT are now attending the sessions together. Latrice was even thinking about going back to school to become an addiction counselor of all things. She was more than qualified for the job.

Granny's death certificate arrived shortly after Yasmin's trial. The official cause of death was "acute hypoxic brain damage", which is what I suspected all along. The fatal injury to her brain occurred as a result of negligent care. There was no need for litigation. The hospital agreed to the thirty million dollar settlement without much of a fight and the money was dispersed evenly among the five surviving siblings.

After all is said and done, I'm convinced.

"The strongest among us are the ones who cry behind closed doors, have the ability to smile through silent pain, and fight battles that are obscured by shame."

CPSIA information can be obtained at www.ICGtesting.com
Printed in the USA
LVOW04s1916161015

458631LV00008B/25/P